The
Morbius
Expedition

By

Leon Michaels

Books by Leon Michaels

The Path Home

From the Mists of Darkness

Task Force Nemesis

Tales From The Bench*

The Hanover Throne

The Echelon Factor

The Morbius Expedition

The Bellus Project

Three Against The Darkness

Random Acts Of Science Fiction

"The Crane Equation Trilogy"

The Crane Equation: The Early Years

The Crane Equation: Rebuilding a Nation

The Crane Equation: The Crane Legacy

"The Black Ops Series"

Operation Damocles

Operation Dokkaebi

Operation Yofune-Nushi

Operation Kartikeya

The Black Orchid

"The Twenty-First Special Operations Group"

Book One: Family

Book Two: Operators

*Contributor & Editor

As always, I must acknowledge the efforts of
My Lovely bride,

In reading and commenting

On my drivel.

My thanks to the writers of several 1950's

Science Fiction stories and movies. If you

Missed what I have stolen from them,

Then I've written it right!!

And to Emerson for the assist.

Cover Photo is from Web Open Source

This is a work of Fiction. Any similarities to individuals past or present is unintentional and purely a coincidence. Any similarities to any individual in the future is pure Karma.

Book One

Starting Point

Lance Corporal Thomas Allan Jenkins kneeled next to the trail he had intersected looking at the footprints in the damp earth. He made out five sets of footprints, but what worried him were two sets of them. One set resembled the print of the footwear the North Vietnamese Army (NVA) wore and another set looked like boots worn by the South Vietnamese Army. The other three sets were sandals which could belong to a variety of individuals, but most likely Viet Cong.

He looked back at the man in the number two position and tapped his arm indicating for his squad leader to come forward. Jenkins was a member of Second Squad, Third Platoon, Kilo Company, Third Battalion, Ninth Marine Regiment also known as Kilo 3/9. His squad had been out on patrol for two days outside Bien Hoa Air Base looking for the folks who had been mortaring the base at night. This was a squad size patrol and so far, all they had found was nothing to make their time worth the effort.

Sergeant Santhon, his squad leader carefully moved to him and watched as Jenkins pointed at the footprints and indicated the differences without speaking. The prints were fresh and the possibility of being heard was too great to even whisper. Ever since Jenkins had joined the squad back on Okinawa before being deployed to Bien Hoa in support of Marine Aircraft Group Twelve (MAG-12), he and Santhon had developed a sort of sign language since Santhon discovered that Jenkins was the best man he had to walk point.

Jenkins touched his nose and acted as if he was sniffing the air and Santhon took a deep breath through his nose and smelled what Jenkins was smelling. It was very faint, but it smelled like smoke mixed with garlic. Santhon signed for Jenkins to find the source of the smoke. Jenkins carefully slipped his pack off and rested it on the jungle floor, then indicated his direction of movement. He was not concerned about his pack as he knew Santhon would have one of the squad towards the rear pick it up for him and bring it to him at the proper time. He carefully moved the selector switch on his M16A1 rifle to full auto, and started his movement through the underbrush parallel to the trail.

Tom Jenkins ability to track and move quietly in thick underbrush came from being raised in Ozark County Missouri where he grew up hunting and fishing in the rugged terrain of the Ozarks. He had grown up stalking food for the dinner table on his family's eighty acres and the surrounding miles of dense terrain.

Slowly he moved, sniffing the air to see if the smell of smoke became stronger, until he heard the chatter of people talking. He looked back at his number two and motioned that he could hear people talking, and that man made the same motion to those following. Jenkins motioned for everyone to stay put as he moved on forward.

He had barely gone thirty feet when an individual dressed as a Viet Cong stepped in front of Tom as he was undoing his pants to urinate. Jenkins shot him, then rose up to see the others in this man's group rising from their sitting positions. Jenkins swept the group with automatic fire from left to right, then back again. He dropped his magazine and quickly inserted another as he moved to the place the men were sitting.

Just as he cleared the brush, he felt a burning sensation on his left thigh as he heard a shot. The man dressed in an NVA uniform had a pistol in his hand firing at Jenkins and Jenkins put a three-round burst in his chest ending the feud. Jenkins looked around the small site to insure no one was moving, then gave a loud, sharp whistle as he continued to watch for anyone else. He had a total of five bodies which matched the count of footprints. Immediately the sound of men rushing forward was heard in the underbrush.

As the squad moved into his location and spread out to insure no one surprised them, Jenkins felt the pain in his thigh increase in intensity. He finally looked down to see blood staining his pants leg and eased the pressure of standing on that leg to the other.

Sergeant Santhon moved to Jenkins and saw the blood on Jenkins leg, then called the attached Navy Corpsman to attend to the wound. As the Corpsman went to work on Jenkins leg, Santhon moved to the bodies, and began stripping everything that might be important to Battalion Intelligence from the bodies, then dumped the packs lying about for anything that might be important.

The Corpsman told Jenkins the bullet was still in his leg, but it had not hit an artery from the way it was bleeding. The Corpsman using the plastic wrapper from the dressing he was going to wrap the wound with and put it over the hole, then pushed a small dirt clod into the hole sealing it, before he carefully wrapped the leg with the dressing. He told Jenkins this would help keep the blood inside the body and infection out. The body would absorb the blood over time.

When Santhon asked the Corpsman about Jenkins wound, the Corpsman said he needed to be medevac'd as soon as possible so the bullet could be removed, and his leg properly fixed up. Santhon checked his map and put them on a route back towards Bien Hoa. He estimated they were seven kilometers from the Air Base, and two from a location where they could be picked up by helicopter. As they moved towards the landing zone, Santhon was on the radio reporting they had been in contact with one wounded, and needed to be picked up.

Jenkins walked in the middle of the squad with the Corpsman following him as he hobbled to the pickup point. As bad as his leg was beginning to hurt, Jenkins knew that the slower he went, the longer they would be exposed. He closed his mind as best he could to the pain and followed the man in front of him.

Seven hours later Jenkins was lying on a bed instead of his cot with fresh sheets, and his leg bound up after having the bullet removed. He had an IV in his arm feeding him enough antibiotics that the Corpsman who checked on him said he could go a year without worrying about catching the clap.

Three days later the Commander of MAG-12 stopped by and presented him with a Purple Heart for his wound. He also told Jenkins the information they had gleaned from the papers and a map found on the bodies helped locate where the mortars and ammunition was being stashed during the daytime that had been used against them.

When Jenkins was released to light duty, he was assigned to work in the Company Supply until stitches were removed and returned to full duty. Two weeks later a Company formation was held, and the MAG-12 Commander pinned a Bronze Star with a 'V' for Valor onto Jenkins uniform for his actions during the patrol. The medal embarrassed him since he figured he was only doing what he had been trained to do, but his Company First Sergeant told him to just wear the medal since it went nice with his Purple Heart.

A month later he was awarded a second Purple Heart when he was hit by a piece of shrapnel while running for a bunker during a rocket attack on the base. Again, Jenkins was lucky in that the wound was not serious enough to send him back to the United States.

Fast Forward

Gunnery Sergeant Thomas Jenkins sat in the office of the First Marine Division Sergeant Major drinking a cup of coffee as the Sergeant Major was talking to him about staying in the Corps.

"Tom, you are an interesting individual. Twenty-two years in the Corps and still only a Gunny. I called Eighth and 'I' about why you were not a First Sergeant, and got a line of bullshit. But they did tell me you were at the top of the promotion list next year. Who have you pissed off during your career?"

Tom chuckled.

"Just about everyone Sergeant Major. Everyone that does not like the fact I don't play politics."

The Sergeant Major looked at Tom's Service Records on his desk and had to chuckle along with him.

"Yeah. You turned down Officer Candidate School twice, Warrant Officer once, all the time while earning your Master's Degree while in service. You're IQ is three points below genius level which makes you smarter than most of the officer's you have served under, yet you get some of the best Fitness Reports I've ever seen. You're PT test scores are on par with men half your age or better, and your range scores are incredible. Why do I suspect you are sandbagging your rifle and pistol qualification scores?"

"Sergeant Major, it's simple. I scored high in boot and have maintained that level ever since, but I also learned that if I improved them too much, I'd find myself either in Sniper School or on the Rifle Team doing nothing but shooting all day. No, I joined the Corps to serve and stayed in to pass my knowledge to the young men and women coming in behind me."

'Tom, I'd love to see the notes attached to your records at Headquarters Marine Corps to see why you have been held back from promotion until you are on the verge of being discharged for being passed over. But the question is, are you really going to retire?"

"Sergeant Major, I extended for Desert Storm and now that we are back home, I think it is time. To be honest, I'm tired of the bullshit out of Washington, and think it's time to hang up my saber and go home."

"Is there anything I can say, or do that can change your mind?"

"Sergeant Major, we have known each other since Okinawa. Do you really think I can be persuaded to change my mind?"

The Sergeant Major laughed.

"No Tom, I seriously doubt it. What are your plans once you are out of the Corps?"

"I have a cousin who is an Under-Sheriff in Oklahoma. He's offered me a job, and I'm considering it."

"Exchange on uniform for another. Not uncommon for a Marine, is it? Tom, can I ask you a personal question?"

"Sure, Sergeant Major."

"Why haven't you ever married?"

Tom took a long drink of coffee and looked past the Sergeant Major at the activity outside his office window before answering.

"I was engaged to a girl I knew back home when you and I first met. She withheld her favors from me telling me it was for our wedding night. I came home, and she was five months pregnant with another boy's child, and they had not married. It seems that every time I find a woman that I would enjoy spending my life with, they make demands on me that I cannot fulfill. So, I just enjoy the ladies that make no demands and cruise through life."

"Rumor is Tom that you are enjoying a Major over at Base Plans and Systems."

"Sergeant Major Santhon, you know that relations between officers and enlisted men are frowned on."

The Sergeant Major laughed.

"Tom, it has been an honor to know and serve with you. You will be missed."

"Sergeant Major, that's the good thing about the Corps, we might be missed, but if we have done our job properly, there is always someone to step in and fill our boots once we depart."

They parted with a handshake and Jenkins returned to Bravo Company, First Battalion, Seventh Marine Regiment where he was the Company Gunny. Sergeant Major Santhon picked up the files on his desk and opened the connecting door to the office of the Commanding General, First Marine Division, and entered to find the General was not alone.

"Sergeant Major Santhon, do you know Colonel Dubasso?"

"No sir I have not had the pleasure, but I certainly know who he is."

Santhon offered his hand which Dubasso took as he spoke.

"Pleasure to meet you Sergeant Major. So, you could not talk Gunny Jenkins into staying in the Corps?"

"No sir, which does not surprise me. He is tired of the chair warmers back in DC screwing with his career. Tom Jenkins is probably the best Marine I ever served with, and he is a better Marine than the majority of First Sergeants, and some Sergeant Majors I know."

"Well Sergeant Major, I think I have a job for him then if he is willing to take it."

"Excuse me Colonel, but what kind of job would NASA have that he could fill? A security guard? That would-be kind of insulting, don't you think?"

Colonel Dubasso laughed.

"Actually, he would be a security guard, but not in the manner you are thinking. From what I have seen of his education records, he took a lot of physics courses, even though his major was in Geography. Plus, he took additional Engineering based courses heavy in mathematics. I bet I could put him in a room full of NASA engineers and he would fit right in. But what NASA has in mind is different, and sorry Sergeant Major, I cannot give you any more than I have already given you."

Sergeant Major Santhon just nodded and returned to his office and the paperwork waiting on his desk. Colonel Dubasso moved to the General's desk and opened the file on Tom Jenkins. He slowly thumbed through the file looking at the entries for a few minutes before closing it up.

"George, is he what you are looking for?" The General asked.

"Yes sir, he is. We have a couple of Special Forces troops and a SEAL we are looking at, but they are officers and still don't have his education and they have other, minor details that he doesn't. From what I understand about Jenkins is that he could probably step into any of those other men's jobs, and do them as well without all the fancy training. Yes, he'll do if we can convince him to take the job."

Later that evening, Tom Jenkins was leaning back against the headboard belonging to Marine Major Joanna Patakia, watching as she brushed her hair out from being wrecked during close bed sheet combat. He had to smile in that she always complained about how he messed her hair up during sex, but would complain if he didn't treat her in the manner in which the hair was messed up.

12

Tom had first met Joanna during what could be characterized as a Cultural Sensitivity Seminar prior to the Division's deployment to Saudi Arabia for Operation Desert Storm. They had several disagreements during the seminar, but both agreed to further exam the others view point.

When Tom returned from Desert Storm, he ran into Joanna in the base gym working out. It was a month after he first saw her that she suggested dinner to further discuss his ideas. Three dinner dates later she invited him to her bed. That was four months ago, and it seemed by this time he had almost moved in with her.

Joanna looked at him from the end of the bed as she brushed her hair.

"Tom, are you sure you want to go back home once you are out of the Corps?"

"Jo, we've talked about this before. If I stay here, I'll end up being just another old Marine sitting in the NCO Club, watching the young Marines pass through wishing I was going with them. Besides, if I stay with you, sooner or later it will affect your career. You've worked too hard to get where you are at, to really risk that beyond what we already have."

They both knew the truth of the matter in that they enjoyed each other in and out of bed, but as enjoyable as it was, there was never a level of love that would be needed to make a life together in their feelings for each other.

On The Table

Tom had said all his goodbyes the day before and spent the night with Joanna. Everything he owned was loaded in the back of his GMC Denali and he planned to leave from her apartment and head for Oklahoma to what the future had laid out for him. He had lived a Spartan life while in the Corps, buying only what he needed and saving every dime he could for the future.

Joanna had already left for her office and he took one last look around the apartment to ensure that he was not leaving anything before placing his key to the apartment on her coffee table and exiting, making sure the door was locked behind him. He was not expecting what greeted him at his truck.

Standing by the driver's door was a Marine Full Colonel in undress Greens.

"Can I help you Colonel?" Tom inquired as he approached.

"Gunny Jenkins, I think you can if you will be kind enough to return to Pendleton with me, so we can talk in a more secure location."

"What's this about Colonel?"

"I would like to offer you a job."

"Colonel Dubasso, unless I've missed something, you work for NASA now, not the Corps."

"Correct Gunny. The job offering is with NASA, and we feel that you are the best candidate for the job."

Jenkins looked at the Colonel for a moment considering what was said about a secure location. What kind of job could a Marine Gunnery Sergeant fill that required a secure location to discuss it?

"Alright Colonel, lead on and I'll let you make your pitch."

"Good. Gunny if we get separated, meet me at the Provost Marshall's office at the CID entrance. We'll use one of their interrogation rooms since they are sound proof."

The Colonel got into a car driven by another man in civilian clothes and they pulled away, so Tom could get out of the parking space. They did get separated because of traffic lights, but the Colonel and his driver were waiting on the sidewalk outside the Provost Marshall's when he pulled into a visitor parking space.

The man with the Colonel was introduced as Jerome Brown, and was a NASA Security Officer. His function at this meeting was to ensure that no recordings were made of the meeting by positioning himself in the recording room during the meeting.

Once in the interrogation room, Colonel Dubasso removed a small DVD player/viewer from his briefcase and set it up for Tom to view. Before he turned it on, he had Tom sign a Non-Disclosure form concerning the briefing he was about to take part in. Tom was handed a pair of earphones, so he would be able to hear every word of the video brief.

As the brief began, Dubasso stepped out of the room then returned with two cups of coffee, sitting one down where Tom could reach it. When the video first came on Tom thought he was watching a Space Program from the Discovery Channel, but it soon became obvious this would never be shown on television.

The video briefing lasted for twenty-seven minutes before it closed. Tom took the earphones off and looked at Dubasso.

"Alright Colonel, let's say I believe this video. What is it that you think I can do for you?"

"Gunny, we need someone with your ability and intelligence to go on this mission as head of security. You have no attachments except a sister whom you rarely see or talk too, and you have never been married. Everyone going on this expedition fits in the same category except that they are scientists, not a warrior."

"And you need a warrior to insure these scientists are able to survive if, and when they land on an inhabitable planet. It has been my experience that people like me are pretty much disliked by the kind of folks you are planning on sending on this expedition."

"I understand what you are saying and even though five of the passengers on the expedition have a military background, none of them are war fighters with your knowledge or experience. NASA can, and has ran the people already picked through several survival courses, but there are some things that cannot be planned for. What if there is animal life that can threaten the expedition? Someone like you will be needed to insure the team's safety."

"The video says the technology has been tested and confirmed for getting us to where ever the trip is headed for. What else is my motivation to go alone on this trip?"

"First of all, you will be a Civil Service employee paid as a GS-15 Step 5 which is equal to my Marine Corps pay and NASA Allowances. Second, you're 401K will be matched in gold as will your savings account, then doubled based upon the price of gold the day you sign on. The day you go into hibernation, all pay up to that point and for a full year after will be included in gold."

"Gold works if I can access it. That's a lot of weight to account for which takes away from other resources for the expedition."

"That's been accounted for based upon the background report on you. Gunny, we have been looking, investigating you since before you deployed to Saudi Arabia. Of all the people we have considered for this job, you are at the top of the list."

"How soon do I have to make a decision?"

"Thirty days. We are on the clock and there are still things you need to be part of, to provide your input into before we have to put everyone into hibernation."

They parted company with Tom carrying three phone numbers in which he could contact Colonel Dubasso. Tom left Camp Pendleton and hit US Interstate 10 and headed east.

Across Southern California and Southern Arizona, he thought about what he had been asked to do. This project was the truth behind Reagan's Star Wars Program. The science had been around for decades, but with money and newer computers, it finally found reality and he was being asked to take part in it. He probably fit the profile for the assignment better than anyone else available.

Ever since he had returned from his first tour in Asia, having been wounded twice and coming home to find the love of his life pregnant with another man's child, Tom had turned his feelings inside to the point some considered him to be a sociopath, except that he always maintained a very outgoing manner when dealing with his troops of either sex.

He thought about Joanna Patakia and wondered if he was an idiot in not staying with her and seeing what life would be like with someone permanent instead of going from one lover to another as he had over the years.

Driving gives a person too much time to think, and he remembered an attractive redhead named Shawna Calloway who he was considering asking to marry him nearly ten years ago until she started pushing him to get out of the Marines. She had finally told him it was either the Marines or her, and he left her standing in her apartment screaming at him as he walked out the door.

He spent the night in Tucson and by the time he reached Las Cruces New Mexico he had made his decision. He contacted Colonel Dubasso who advised him to head for Houston and the Johnson Space Center.

Houston, You Have A Problem

For the first three days, Tom went through getting measured for his different space suits and his hibernation suit. He had an office which he was rarely in those days with sign on the door saying he was a Geographer based upon his Master's Degree. It was a fairly open-ended title without being specific about his real purpose of providing security for the crew.

There were twenty-four in the crew broken down between twelve males and twelve females. Considering the distance of the flight and knowing they will be the only humans on a new planet without the ability to return to Earth, each individual understood that they would be the beginning of the human race on their target planet.

Tom looked at the list of survival equipment and weapons for the expedition and had them laid out on the floor of a conference room. The actual items he was looking at were a complete extra set of the items, as the main items were already packed and loaded in a module attached to their space craft. He was amazed how stupid people could be with such high IQ's and education.

Colonel Dubasso entered the room and side stepped the equipment on the floor as he walked to where Tom was sitting on a table looking at the equipment list on a clipboard.

"What's up Gunny?"

"Colonel, did you have anything to do with this bullshit?"

Dubasso looked at the items on the floor then at Tom.

"No Gunny, this was done by NASA. What's the problem?"

"Half this shit is pure junk. It might be alright for twenty-four to forty-eight hours in a temperate climate, but worthless if in a jungle or artic climate. Beyond forty-eight hours forget it. Plus, the blades are too flimsy."

Tom held up a survival sheath knife which he had broken the blade about an inch from the tip.

"Who decided a ceramic blade was suitable for survival?"

"Honestly Tom, I don't know, but this is a real problem considering everyone's survival pack is already loaded on the vehicle."

"Same with the weapons?"

"Yes, those are already loaded on your excursion vehicle. You see a problem with them?"

"Whose idea is the Barrett 50 Cal?"

"The committee determined if you ran up against a large, dangerous creature this would be the best to insure crew safety."

"The committee? Why am I not surprised? Listen, if we do run up against a large creature requiring a fifty, don't you think I might need more than one hundred rounds of ammunition?"

"Tom, I don't know what to say here."

"Colonel, I'm looking at a pile of crap here which will cause myself and others a lot of heartache. If I was the suspicious type, I'd say someone has set this expedition up to fail."

"Gunny Jenkins do you realize what you are saying?"

"I said if I was the suspicious type, but what I think is some desk bound expert did the picking based on price and some magazine article that was written for pay, and not for reliability."

"What do you suggest we do Gunny?"

"Well if we were going up to the vehicle awake, I'd say we take up replacement gear and jettison what is worthless. But if I was you I'd contact the nearest Nav Air unit and have their folks build survival pack to cover every environment we might encounter. But the weapons are going to be a real problem."

"How so?"

"The M9 Beretta is a piece of shit. The ammo is 115 grain full metal jacket when it should be 124 or 147 grain weights. A mix of hollow point and FMJ's would work, but the 115 does not have the stopping power we might need. Hell, a good .357 Magnum would be a lot better. How well did the women handle the Beretta in training?"

"Not as well as we had hoped for, but they did qualify with them. What would you suggest?"

"They Sig Arms P239 is a single stack and we can get it in the .40 caliber Smith & Wesson. A 155-grain bullet will do better than the 115-grain bullet the 9mm is pushing. Grip is smaller, but we'd need to test the women with it."

"I can probably arrange the test part, but we'd still have to deal with the additional weight."

"Yeah and I haven't gotten to the best part yet. If I was going to pick a battle rifle to take with me on a trip like this, it wouldn't be the M16A2. I'd take an AK-47. It has better penetration and is not as delicate to the environment as the M-16."

"Shit Gunny. We should have brought you in on this two years ago."

Tom just looked at the Colonel as the Colonel looked at the mess on the floor.

"Okay Gunny what else?"

"I'd have to go through the entire manifest to find any other problems. The survival rifles are alright, but I'd like a twelve gauge along for the ride. Interchangeable barrels for defense or hunting just to name one more item that would be nice to have."

"Alright, if you don't have anything else remember, you meet the rest of the crew at 1500 hours. Are you going to say anything to them about this mess?"

"No, not my place. Look Colonel, we can make do with this crap if push comes to shove, but I'd like better odds at the table."

"I'll see what I can do, but we have to watch the weight."

"I understand. You know, a 300 Winchester Magnum would probably do as well as the fifty caliber Barrett, and it would be a third of the weight in weapon alone plus maybe five times the ammo in the overall weight package."

"Sergeant Major Santhon said you were strange man. You are upset about what you are seeing spread out on the floor here, and yet it seems that you'll still go along for the ride without complaint."

"I've made my complaint Colonel. Since I have no authority to change this mess, and I've signed on for the ride, all I can do now is move on and hope for the best."

"Why do I have the feeling you are plotting to change or fix things before the launch."

"You are a very perceptive individual Colonel. Plotting and accomplishing are two separate creatures in the herd."

Colonel Dubasso chuckled as he left Tom to ponder what he had to do to fix what others had messed up.

Tom just shook his head at what he was seeing knowing that there were over thirty thousand rolls of toilet paper with each roll vacuum sealed and being used in every module as padding. Thirty thousand rolls of toilet paper, and they spent good money on the crap he was looking at on the floor.

He could only shake his head and return to his office for the time being.

Meeting the Crew

During the time Tom was at the Center, he had kept his office door closed as he read the files on the other members of the crew, and the manifest for the equipment he was responsible for. He had passed several of his crewmates in the halls over the week, but had yet to interact with any of them.

Because of his position on the crew, he had access to everyone's psych report along with their complete NASA files and personal records of military personal in the crew. By the time he was to be introduced to the crew, he knew more about them then they knew about each other. He also knew which crew members were already pairing up even if it was only for a trial before launch.

The Mission Commander and Command Pilot for this mission was Navy Captain Richard J. Youngerford. He graduated from the University of Washington with a degree as an Aerospace Engineer. He had twenty combat missions during Vietnam and three shuttle flights under his belt. He was an African-American.

Second in command of the mission and pilot was Air Force Colonel Jeffery M. Dunback. He was a graduate of the Air Force Academy with a degree in Engineering. He had flown the F-117 Nighthawk before joining NASA.

Doctor Robert L. Grey was a graduate of Texas A&M with a degree in Animal Husbandry and a Veterinarian. This would be his first mission in space.

Doctor James A. Ostrow was a Neurosurgeon having graduated from the University of Houston. This would be his first mission.

Roger T. Lindstrom had a Master's Degree in Mechanical Engineering from the University of Tulsa. He had his own consulting firm before being recruited by NASA for this mission.

Peter J. Moran was a Civil Engineer from Ohio State University. He had worked for NASA for ten years and this was also his first mission.

Doctor Michael Lathrop was Geologist from the University of Arizona where he also taught Geology before coming to NASA for this mission.

Miguel Ortega had a Master's Degree in Electrical Engineer from Purdue. He had worked for NASA since graduating Purdue and had one shuttle mission behind him. He was a Second Generation Mexican-American.

Paul McCabe was a graduate of Stanford with a degree in Computer Design Engineering. He was recruited from Microsoft for this mission.

U.S. Navy Chief Wallace T. Green was a Heavy Equipment Specialists in the SeaBee's prior to being recruited for this mission.

U.S. Navy Chief Andrew A. Sharpe was a SeaBee Machinist also recruited for this mission. He was an African-American.

Doctor Asami Y. Nakajima, Medical Doctor. Trained in Internal Medicine at John Hopkins and was a resident at Hopkins when recruited for this mission. She was a third generation Japanese American.

Doctor Raelyn S. Silvers graduated from the University of Iowa where she also taught Horticulture. She was recruited for this mission. She was Native-American.

Doctor Christa J. Nichols was a Doctor of Astro-Physics from Princeton who had worked for NASA since graduating. She had one shuttle mission behind her.

Doctor Nadia A. Konoval was a Biologists graduating from the University of Nebraska. Recruited for this mission.

Lauren D. Randall had a Master's Degree in Chemical Engineering from Purdue. She was working for Shell Oil when recruited for this mission.

U.S. Army Chief Warrant Officer Three Karen L. Costello was a Physician's Assistant trained at the University of Maryland and was assigned to Walter Reed Hospital when recruited for this mission.

Mia J. Lathan was a Meteorologists with a Bachelors' Degree from the University of Oklahoma working for NOAA when recruited for this mission. She was African-American.

Sarah J. Thomas had a Master's Degree in Communications from Stanford. She had worked for NASA/JPL before coming on board for this mission.

Doctor Jayne L. Martin was a Dentist with her degree from the University of Oregon. She was a junior partner in a practice in Portland when recruited for this mission.

Doctor Patrice E. Grant was a graduate of MIT in Environmental Engineering. She was working for NASA on loan back to MIT when recruited to the mission.

Doctor Emily J. Turner was an Ophthalmologist working at John Hopkins with her degree from the University of Florida. She was further schooled as an Optometrist for this mission.

Doctor Deanna L. Howell was a Psychologist with her degree from USC where she also taught Psychology. She was African-American.

One aspect of the mission and the reason why the ratio between male and female was even, was so once out of hibernation and on the ground, it was hoped couples would form and begin the process of populating the planet. All the females were in their early to mid-thirties and in prime physical condition for the mission.

Tom decided to have a bit of fun at today's meeting and see what played out from his appearance. He knew he was not what many women called handsome, but the years of weight training to stay in shape to perform his missions as a Marine gave him a body builder's form. He changed shirts putting on a NASA logoed Polo shirt that was one size too small which caused the material to tightly form across his chest and his biceps to completely fill his short sleeves.

What Tom was wanting to see was if any of the females who had been paring up with the men made any moves on him. He had no particular female in mind at this time, since Joanna was still haunting his mind at times, but he wanted to see how serious those pairings were before hibernation. Tom had no intention of taking any of those females to bed, but would consider the others if he felt the need, and was comfortable with them after getting to know them.

Tom knew exactly how long it would take to go from his office to the classroom where the meeting would take place, so he waited until the last minute, so he would not interact with the others as they filed into the classroom.

Just as Tom turned the corner to the hallway to the classroom, he saw the last crew member enter the classroom and the security guard in the hallway close the door. Tom walked up to the guard, showed his NASA ID card which the guard checked against a roster, then opened the door so Tom could enter the room.

Tom just slipped in and stood against the wall by the door surveying the scene. The classroom would seat seventy-five people and the first two rows were taken up with the crew. Three rows behind the crew were five people sitting down with Colonel Dubasso leaning over a table talking to one of them. Dubasso looked up to see Tom and nodded before leaving the conversation he was having with the gentleman he was talking too.

Dubasso moved to the podium in front of the classroom.

"Ladies and Gentlemen, we now have a name for our project and the final crew member. The powers to be have determined that this project will be called The Morbius Expedition. Named after the character Doctor Morbius in the movie Forbidden Planet. Not sure why it was picked, but let's hope the expedition turns out better than the Doctor did in the movie."

He signaled for Tom to come forward.

"Now for the last crew member."

Everyone turned to watch as Tom moved from the back of the room to stand beside the podium and Colonel Dubasso.

"Ladies and gentlemen, this is Master Gunnery Sergeant Thomas Jenkins, Marine Corps retired, who has been selected to go on the expedition as the head of security."

Tom never looked at Dubasso when he commented about his rank knowing that it would be explained to him later.

"For those of you that are not aware of what a Marine Master Gunnery Sergeant is, they are equal in rank to Sergeant Majors except they get their hands dirty where Sergeant Majors mostly deal with administrative matters. Master Gunnery Sergeant Jenkins is highly trained and just to let you know he has the second highest IQ on the crew. Remember the charter for the expedition, in that the head of security has the final word concerning crew safety from this day forward. His decisions overrule the flight commander except in the matters of flight. This was highly debated during the formation of the expedition and was the criteria in selecting the head of security."

Dubasso stepped away from the podium.

"Tom, please introduce yourself to the crew."

Tom took the podium.

"Thank you Colonel Dubasso. As the Colonel said my name is Thomas or Tom if you wish. If you wish to use my Marine Corps title, then let's shorten it to just Gunny which I will readily respond too. I was not expecting to address the crew in this manner, but if anyone has a question, ask it."

A hand was raised on the front row.

"Yes, Doctor Nakajima?"

She gave him an odd look knowing that there were no name plates on the tables in front of them to tell a stranger who they were addressing.

"Yes, where are you from? Originally that is."

"I was born and raised in Ozark County Missouri, about twenty miles from the Arkansas state line."

"Thank you, Gunny."

"You're welcome Doctor Nakajima. Any other questions?"

Another hand was raised.

"Yes, Chief Green."

"Gunny, have you had a chance to go over our survival equipment yet?"

"Interesting question Chief. Yes, I have, and I suspect by your question you also have some doubts about the equipment."

"Yeah, I do, but since I have no expertise in such things, I just kept quiet."

"First of all, Chief, I would have told you to speak out and speak out loud about that pile of garbage I spent two days going through. I have already voiced my opinions concerning it, and have been told it is already aloft and in position with our vehicle."

He paused noticing the people at the back of the crew were acting a bit nervous.

"People, we have thirty days before we go to sleep. Each of us are allotted two hundred kilos of personal property on this voyage. I will publish a list of items I feel each person should add to that property list to replace those items already packed that I feel is not serviceable for a mission such as this. I have already given my comments on how or why those items were selected to Colonel Dubasso, so I will not repeat myself here. Two hundred kilos is a lot of weight, and I'm sure each of you could probably exchange twenty or thirty kilos if it means your chances of survival is increased. Any other questions?"

He waited for a moment and no hands were raised.

"Captain Youngerford, you are the mission commander and I have no wish to usurp your authority, but I will advise you on all matters concerning crew safety. I'll only insist on safety items once we are on the ground. It's your ship Sir."

"Thank you, Gunny, that thought did cross my mind."

"Any other questions?"

He looked at the faces looking up at him and smiled.

"Miss Costello, the look on your face tells me you have a question, but are not sure how to ask it."

She moved around in her chair and looked around the room before commenting.

"Gunny Jenkins, this is the first time we have laid eyes on you, but it seems you know each of our names by face. How long have you been in Houston?"

"I've been here a week now and because I am Head of Security, I have had access to your files. I just studied the files matching faces on the photographs in the files with your names."

"So, you're that smart then?"

"Miss Costello, I am not qualified to say if I am or not. My test scores say I am, but maybe I just got lucky in guessing parts of the test. I do have a knack for remembering people and their names which played out well today don't you think?"

She laughed and nodded.

"Anything else? If not Colonel Dubasso the podium is yours Sir."

Dubasso took the podium as Tom took a seat on the second row. Tom knew he had just created waves in the program with his statement, but Chief Green had opened the door for him to comment and there was no time to sugar coat things.

"Well people are there any comments about what Gunny Jenkins has informed us about your survival equipment?" Dubasso inquired of the audience. Several people looked over at Tom, but no one spoke up.

"Alright then. Doctor Pritchard do you have anything to say?"

Doctor Pritchard was sitting behind Tom and just shook his head no. Pritchard was the project manager for the Morbius Expedition, and ultimately responsible for every kilo of weight and every item being taken on the expedition.

"Okay then. People we have thirty days to finish up and get ready for the mission. You have the training schedule already so let's get this done."

As the others were standing, Tom rose and just moved to the door when he heard his name. He turned to find Doctor Pritchard coming up to him.

"Yes, Doctor Pritchard?"

"We need to talk."

"Certainly Doctor. What's on your mind?"

"Not here."

"Doctor, if this is about my comments concerning crew safety, then in front of the crew is the best place for such a conversation since it greatly affects them."

Tom could see the crew lining up behind Doctor Pritchard to exit the room, and could hear his comments about crew safety. Pritchard turned around to see the crew standing behind him, waiting for his response to Tom's comment. Tom knew Pritchard did not want to have his comments out in the open by the look on his face.

"Doctor Pritchard, if this is about the mission budget, I'll make you a deal. Based on my contract, I will be taking over a million dollars in gold on the trip. Just to make things simple, that is over thirteen hundred kilos of dead weight which is not included in my authorized two hundred kilos of personal property. Now unless the planet we end up on is inhabited, why do I need that much gold? Even if the inhabitants utilize gold, I'm sure our arrival will be more valuable to them than our gold will be. I'll pay for all the new equipment out of my funds, give the rest to the Navy Relief Fund then only take say, fifty kilos of gold. That reduces the lift weight immensely, plus insures the crew has what it needs to survive on a desolate planet."

"Well Mister Jenkins that was a concern." Pritchard replied.

"Gunny, I'll kick in on that idea." Captain Youngerford spoke up from behind Pritchard.

Pritchard turned to see the entire crew nodding their agreement, and from what he could see and hear all of them agreed with the concept. He turned back to address Tom.

"Mister Jenkins, how soon can you put together your list of items?"

"It's on my desk right now. May I suggest that the extra weight be used to increase the volume of emergency rations?"

Pritchard just nodded his acceptance to the new concept. Tom looked at the crew then Pritchard.

"Doctor Pritchard, we do need to sit down and work out the weight problems. May I suggest that each crew member submit their weight reductions to you then we can work out the details, but time is short, and we cannot delay obtaining what we need to survive?"

"Yes, yes the quicker the better." Pritchard agreed.

Tom looked at the crew once again then turned away to the door. He could hear people talking behind him about what they could do without as he exited the door and went to his office. He sat down at his desk and wondered if he had made the right decision, but as he had always done in his life, he made a decision and lived with the final results.

Pritchard stopped by Tom's office a few minutes later and Tom just held out the list he had made up for him to take.

"Mister Jenkins, you put me in a very uncomfortable position in the classroom."

"Doctor Pritchard, do you have a problem in calling me Tom or even Gunny? But as far as putting you in an uncomfortable position, I did not do that, you did that to yourself. You could have waited five minutes then stopped by here and we could have had that conversation in private. So, consider this, we have thirty days to fix what is broken and after that, you will never have to see or listen to me again."

"I don't think I like your attitude."

"Doctor Pritchard if everything works as designed, you will be dead eons before we wake up to land on an inhabitable planet. The decisions you have made here will affect our chances of survival, yet you will never know if we succeeded or failed in our mission. Get control of your ego and get with the program Doctor. Your fame will come from a successful launch, not a successful mission. That part belongs to the crew and the crew alone."

"I've been part of this mission since the very beginning over a decade ago, and you come in here and criticize the work we have put into it."

"Doctor Pritchard, I am only qualified to comment on a very minor part of the mission. One that affects the lives of the crew once the mission has reached its final stage. I can imagine the stress you are under to complete this mission, especially since we now have a president who would love to close NASA down and use the funds for his feel-good programs. My goal is to insure the success of the mission, not to downplay all the work others have put into it. As I said before, get a grip on your ego and let's get the show on the road."

Pritchard just glared at Tom before leaving with Tom's list in his hand. Tom returned to reading the expedition's material manifest. He had only been back to reading when he felt a presence and looked up at the door. Standing in the doorway was a moderately attractive black woman.

"What can I do for you Doctor Howell?"

"Please call me Deanna or Dee is fine. Gunny, I heard what you said to Pritchard, careful with him. He has a small man complex and does not like being put in his place."

"Deanna, I have dealt with people like him before. But I thank you for the warning. Is that the only reason you stopped by?"

"I suppose you know the reason why the ratio between male and female is equal on this expedition?"

"Yes Deanna, and for your information I'm color blind. I only look at the interior of a person, not their exterior. The color of their skin does not determine if they are a good or bad person."

"What's your criteria for making such a determination?"

"I guess you are going to have to discover that on your own as will the other ladies of the expedition."

"So, you'll have no problem having dinner with me tonight?"

"Deanna, my last lover is darker than you are. She is a Major in the Corps and asked me to stay with her after I retired. If she was not a serving officer I would have considered it, but at this stage in her career, being associated with me, a white enlisted man would have been detrimental to her career. We barely kept our relationship a secret as it was, but she is too good an officer to suffer because of me."

"It sounds like you really cared for her."

"I suppose I do, otherwise I would not have entered into the relationship I had with her."

"How are you going to adjust to this arrangement on the Expedition?"

"Deanna I'm a pragmatist. In time, we'll all go to sleep and if everything works out, the next day we'll awaken and start our lives all over again. But the reality is the Joanna will have died long before I awaken, and there is nothing I can do about that under these circumstances. So, I'll wake up and move on with my life."

"Interesting philosophy on life, but you never answered my question concerning dinner."

Tom lightly laughed.

"Dinner with you sounds like an enjoyable evening. Since we are all living in training apartments do we eat in or out?"

"I'm a lousy cook, so how about out?"

"Fine with me. Let's say I collect you at your apartment at six-thirty, and I'll let you pick the restaurant since you have asked me out."

Deanna laughed as she turned and walked out of his office. Tom figured this would be happening during the remaining time before going into hibernation since the women had almost a year with the others, while he was the new man in the crew. He thought about Joanna and knew in his heart he was right in his decision concerning her. He could not find what he considered love for her, but he did care for her enough to let her go, and hoped she had a wonderful life.

That afternoon Tom went through his final fitting of his hibernation suit and his hard suit for extra-vehicular activity. Once his hard suit was finished, he would go through a week in the pool learning how to work in the suit in case he had to go out of the vehicle for some repair or recovery work.

Tom picked up Deanna Howell exactly at the time he stated, and she said she wanted to go to an Italian restaurant she had heard about from one of the NASA personal. The meal was enjoyable as they just talked with Deanna mostly asking questions about his life as a Marine, and even approached his status of never marrying. They were drinking coffee at the end of the dinner when she opened a topic that Tom had expected.

"Tom, this might be rushing into things, but I have not been with a man in nearly two months. I noticed a motel down the street and I wonder if we might make use of it tonight?"

Tom put his cup down and smiled at her.

"No Deanna, we shall not, and I'll explain why. First, I am interested in why a woman who was a lesbian signed up for a mission such as this where she has committed to basically becoming a baby factory once the expedition establishes a colony."

"How do you know about my past life?"

"As I said in the meeting I have access to everyone's files. Which also makes me wonder why you were recruited based upon your life style at the time of recruitment. But then again, you and Pritchard both went to USC, did you not?"

"Go on Tom."

"So far you have slept with five of the male crew and two of the females who are listed as bi-sexual. Based upon many of the questions you have asked me tonight and your background, I suspect you are preparing a paper on the psychology of people who know they will never see earth again, which in some ways a guarantee of death in many ways. Then I have to ask myself why a person like you is so ready to take that journey never knowing if their paper is accepted or denied."

He just sat looking at her as she moved her coffee cup around pondering his statements. She finally looked directly at him as she answered.

"Yes, Roland Pritchard and I went to USC and he recruited me for this mission for several reasons. One was in fact to write a paper which could be used to assist in selection of people to hopefully follow us and establish a stable colony on another world."

She picked her cup up and took a sip before continuing.

"He also learned that my professional career was waning, and I was in trouble of losing my tenure at USC as a professor. I crossed a line with a student which I am at fault with. Was that in my file?"

"No Deanna, it was not. Most likely Pritchard arranged for that part to be kept out of your file. So, what is left I should know?"

"I lost my virginity in high school and enjoyed a decent sex life through my sophomore year in college. By that time, I was bi-sexual, then I fell in love with a jock who used me up then dumped me. I never looked back as I moved to making love to women only. Until I joined the crew, I had not been with a man during those years. Funny thing about that is I really enjoy being with a man, but not the pain of being used then rejected by one. It's only funny in that I have been hurt just as bad by a woman, yet I never left that life until Pritchard came along to rescue me from ruining my career and my life."

"Deanna, I suppose tonight is just a paragraph or two for your paper."

"Yes, it is. Even the sex would have been included in a fashion. I'll not apologize for my intentions."

Tom looked into his own coffee cup, then pushed it aside.

"I really wonder what the truth is behind Pritchard recruiting you, but at this point it really doesn't matter. Where ever we end up we'll not have the luxury of finding another partner if things between two people does not work out. Deanna, I did not join this expedition thinking I'd find the love of my life, because I just might have left her in San Clemente if I had allowed it to happen. But one thing I am sure of is that you will never know what I am like in a bed. What you do with others is your business, but if you interfere at all with my own life, you will regret it. I mean you no harm, but will insure that you will remember me till your last breath decades later."

Tom stood, took a money clip from his pocket, tossed a couple bills on the table, then offered his hand to Deanna. She looked at the hand, then up at him. There were tears slowly moving down her cheeks as she took his hand and stood. He acted the perfect gentleman as he escorted her to his Denali, assisted her in getting seated then driving back to the apartment complex.

Neither spoke during the drive home until Tom pulled into his parking space in front of the complex.

"Tom, Pritchard has been using me as a spy, telling him things that are not in the daily reports. And before you ask no, I am not sleeping with him. He has tried a couple times to get me in bed, but I've kept that distance. You embarrassed him in public, so watch yourself around here."

Deanna got out of the truck before Tom could get out and he watched her quickly walk away towards her side of the apartment complex. He often hated himself because he had the tendency of speaking his mind at times he should just stay quiet. Maybe a sweaty night with Deanna would help his own problems of leaving Joanna, then again it might have made things worse.

He walked towards his side of the complex and caught the glimpse of a man standing in the shadows near the entrance. Was this someone sent by Pritchard to cause him harm or just someone outside taking the night air? As he got closer the individual stepped from the shadows and stepped in his way. It was Paul McCabe, the crew's Computer Engineer.

"Need something Mister McCabe?"

"What are your intentions concerning Deanna Howell?"

"None what so ever Mister McCabe. She and I could not find common grounds to take the dinner tonight any further than dessert."

Tom could see the tension in McCabe's body ease up and he seemed to relax. He waited for a long moment for McCabe to speak and when he did not respond to his answer, Tom gave him some relief.

"Paul, if you want her, go to her. I'd say she could use the company tonight."

"What did you do to her?"

"Nothing at all, we just talked. But she needs a friend now, and I'm not that friend."

McCabe looked at him then walked past Tom heading for Deanna's apartment. Tom never looked back as he went to his own apartment.

In The Pool

Tom was in the pool training to replace an antenna with Miguel Ortega, the crew's Electrical Engineer. This was his third time in the pool training in as close a zero-gravity atmosphere in the awkward hard suit. The job was nearly done when he began to feel light headed. He checked his wrist data display and his oxygen level was correct as was his CO_2 level, yet he knew something wasn't right.

He pushed back from the antenna he had been bolting in place and began to give the emergency hand signal to the rescue divers in the pool with them. Almost immediately he felt the safety line hooked to his back began to lift him to the surface as his vision began to become fuzzy. Tom tried to punch up more oxygen on his wrist control, but could not focus.

His head was beginning to hurt as was his chest as he cleared the water and was moved over to the deck and placed into his suit bracket stand. He was immediately attended to by the technicians at poolside and in seconds they had his helmet off him as he was gasping for breath. Just as he blacked out he felt an oxygen mask being placed on his face and felt the dry oxygen issuing from the mask for him to breath.

Tom woke in the infirmary with a major headache and his chest still hurting. He tried to raise his head, but was weak and just lay still with an oxygen mask firmly strapped to his head. He looked to his right to see an IV in his arm, then as his eyes began to work better could see Doctor Nakajima working on a chart.

"Doc." He croaked out.

Nakajima looked over at him then stepped to him.

"Be quiet Gunny, you have a near miss today. Let your body take care of itself."

"What happened?"

"According to Andy Sharpe, someone tied a tank of Argon gas into your oxygen supply line. Since Argon is inert and is heavier than oxygen, it displaced the oxygen in your lungs. Another minute and you would have died at the bottom of the pool."

"Sabotage?"

"Colonel Dubasso thinks so. Just relax, you should be up and about in a couple of hours."

"Thanks, Asami."

"You're welcome Tom."

Tom knew there was only one person at the Space Center that might want him injured or dead, but it would be very difficult to prove it. As he lay there, he had to consider the effect on the crew in that would they now be worried about the status of the mission and their own part in it.

"Doc?"

"Yes Tom."

"Get me Paul McCabe."

"You can talk to him later, once you are better."

"No Asami, now. This concerns the mission."

"Alright Tom, but try to rest."

He heard Doctor Nakajima talk on a phone requesting Paul McCabe to report to the Infirmary as he just tried to relax as the fog in his head cleared and the ache in his chest slowly subsided. Tom had no idea how long he lay there before Paul McCabe entered the room and spoke to Nakajima. She told him to the Gunny wanted to talk to him.

"Gunny, you wanted to see me?"

"Yeah. First if they are not part of the crew, run them out of the room and close the door."

"It's just you, me and Asami in the room, but let me close the door."

"Doc?"

"Yes Tom?"

"Are there any recording devices in the room such as monitors and microphones?"

'Yes, why?"

"Disconnect them before I discuss anything with Paul."

"Why?"

"Please Asami, just do as I ask."

"Okay Gunny, give me a couple minutes. Paul, give me a hand, will you?"

A few minutes later both McCabe and Nakajima were standing beside Tom's bed.

"Okay Gunny, what's up?" McCabe asked.

"I understand you helped write the mission software."

"Yeah, I did, about forty percent of it, and I have gone over it a couple times to make sure I'm familiar with it."

"How hard would it be to tamper with the software?"

"Tamper with it? What are you saying?"

"What if someone wanted this mission to fail? For us to go to sleep and never wake up? How hard would it be to do that through the software?"

"Shit Gunny, are you saying someone is trying to sabotage the mission?"

Tom just looked at him without answering.

"I get it now Gunny. Alright, I'll get right on it."

"Thanks Paul. Get with Colonel Dubasso and tell him what I have asked you to do. Keep it low keyed and if any flack comes back at you, send them to me. This concerns crew safety meaning it's on my shoulders."

"I understand Gunny. Now get back on your feet, I owe you a beer for the other night."

"No problem Paul. Just be careful. In fact, grab Wallace Green and tell him I would appreciate it if he watches your back while working. Tell him everything he needs to know."

"Will do. I'll let you know if I find anything."

McCabe left leaving Tom alone with Doctor Nakajima as he felt his body recovering from the near asphyxiation caused by the entrance of the Argon gas into his oxygen supply system. He just lay there with Nakajima checking his vital signs and the blood oxygen sensor information attached to his finger.

Tom closed his eyes and just relaxed to the point he went to sleep until he was awakened by Nakajima taking the oxygen mask off his face. She leaned over him and checked his eye reaction with a penlight before standing up and began to remove his IV.

"Thanks Doc."

"Tom, you scared the heck out of me, but how did you know you were in trouble? Argon asphyxiation usually hits fast."

"Oxygen deprivation when diving creates similar effects. I may have never gone through the Combat Diver's Course, but I have been scuba diving for years. But I must admit this hit me quicker than I realized. Whoever tied that line into my supply would have been successful if they had opened the valve a bit more."

"Well I'm glad they failed?"

"Any particular reason Asami?"

She just reached over and touched the side of his face then went back to the chart she had on him to make some more notes. Tom looked at her and smiled to himself. Was her concern for a crew member or was there something else to consider? She was an attractive woman with a modest figure typical of Asian women.

Asami checked the oxygen sensor data, removed it from his finger than pulled the sheet down from his chest before she removed the heart monitor contacts then wiped the sticky tape residue from his chest. Tom reached up, took one of her hands and brought it to his lips then kissed it.

"Thanks again Asami."

She smiled at him, then pulled her hand from his and went back to work cleaning him up. When she finished she stood back from the bed and leaned against the counter.

"Tom, this is neither the time nor place, but if you ask me to dinner in a couple of days, I just might accept the invite."

"Then I just might invite you to dinner in a couple days so brace yourself for the shock."

Asami laughed.

"Tom, one of the suit techs brought your clothes while you were out. They are on the chair by the door. I'm going to step out so take your time getting up and getting dressed. I'll be outside if you need me."

"I noticed Karen Costello wasn't here, or any nurses."

"Karen is in a surgical course and I sent the regular nurses out once we had you laid out and under control. And before you ask, no I did not strip you, the para-medics did that and took your sensor suit back with them to the techs."

"Well that's good cause I hate to be laughed at while unconscious and nude."

Asami laughed again the walked out of the room closing the door behind her. Tom took his time as he was weak, but was able to get dressed without asking for help. When he opened the door, Asami was standing at the nurse's station waiting for him with a wheelchair. He walked over to her and realized this was the first time he had been this close to her with both standing. He stood six foot-one and her head never came to his shoulders.

"What's that for Asami?"

"You get to ride back to your apartment where you will spend the rest of the day resting from your adventure."

Tom just smiled and sat down in the wheelchair. Asami pushed him down the hall to the exit and once they were outside he made another comment concerning his adventure in the pool.

"Asami something I nearly forgot. My instrument pad did not register any problem with my oxygen supply. Could that have been a natural occurrence or were my sensors tampered with?"

"I can't say Tom, but I'll get someone to look into that. Maybe Lauren Randall since she is a Chemical Engineer. Maybe she'd know."

"Okay, thanks. Man, that took a lot out of me."

"You're lucky to be alive. If the pool techs had not gotten your helmet off as quick as they did, you might have survived, but only the gods would know what damage it could have done, especially to your brain."

"That thought has crossed my mind Asami. I suspect I have upset someone, but there is also something else bothering me, yet I cannot get a handle on it."

"What would that be Tom?"

"As I said, I cannot get a handle on it. Anyway, I'll follow my doctor's orders and get some rest. Am I allowed to go back to work tomorrow?"

"Yes, but nothing strenuous for at least forty-eight hours."

"Oh, until we go to dinner?"

Asami stopped pushing him as he turned his head back to look at her.

"Damn, I stepped into that one, didn't I?"

"Yes Asami, you did, but I was just pulling your chain."

"Yeah well, keep that in mind, besides you have not asked me out so there."

"Doctor Asami Nakajima, would you do me the honor of stepping out to a nice dinner and hopefully pleasant conversation the day after tomorrow?"

"Master Gunnery Sergeant Thomas Jenkins, I will consider your request and will let you know if it is feasible to be seen with you in public."

"Feasible? Don't you mean advisable?"

"Either way, I do believe you are trouble."

"Asami, seriously if you have reconsidered your earlier statement about going to dinner with me, I have no problem with you saying no."

Asami never said another word to him until she finally had him back at his apartment. She turned back to him as she was about to exit with the wheelchair.

"Tom, I have not been with a man since reporting for this mission, and I'm not into women. I have no intention of allowing our dinner to end up in bed. I just want to get to know you away from this madness."

"Asami, I have never tried to seduce a woman into my bed. I have always felt if that is where she wants to be, then she will make the move in that direction. I have no problem just spending the evening with an attractive woman, a good meal and polite conversation."

"Thank you, Tom. Now get some rest. Good evening."

"Good evening Asami."

After he locked the apartment door, Tom went to his closet and removed a bag from it and took it to his bed. From the bag he took out an Ithaca 1911 Pistol that was once property of the US Government before it was replaced by the M9 Beretta. Also from the bag he removed a box of two hundred and twenty-five grain Federal Hydro-Shok Jacketed Hollow Point ammunition and loaded three magazines. After he inserted and chambered a round into the 1911, he removed the magazine and replaced the one round he had chambered giving him eight rounds in the pistol.

After he put the bag back in the closet and placed the pistol and magazines on his nightstand he laid down and just stared at the ceiling. What was he missing in the equation that placed him in the hospital? Was Pritchard's ego so fragile that he would actually try to kill him for the embarrassment he had caused? There had to be something else in the equation. Some unknown variable that needed discovered before it was too late.

Jade Green

Tom got up early as he normally did, dressed for a run, but this time he put on a lightweight windbreaker with a tanker holster under it with the 1911 tucked away in it. The first mile took a lot out of him as he purged the remains of the Argon from his lungs, then he began to feel better by the end of the second mile.

Half way into his third mile he came upon a group of runners that turned out to be part of the crew. Asami was in this group and called out to him as he passed them. He slowed down and let her catch up.

"Tom, how are you feeling?"

"Doc, the first mile was tough until my lungs cleared by the end of the mile. Doing good now. Thanks for asking."

"Well take it easy anyway. You came real close to a body bag."

"Understand Asami. I'll finish this mile and hit the weights before breakfast."

"Again, take it easy. Watch the weights as you still may have some infusion of Argon within the tissue."

"Good advice Doc, I'll watch out and start light."

Tom ran on as his normal pace then did as he told Asami about shutting down. In the weight room he reduced his normal weights twenty percent then slowly built back up to them. When he looked into the mirror on the wall after setting the free weights back into their rack he saw Asami watching him. He smiled at her image in the mirror and she smiled back before moving over to a Bow Flex and arranged the rods to the desired weight.

He left a few minutes later as he finished up his routine. Tom also wanted to get away from Asami as she was becoming a distraction. He had no illusion of romance between them, but she was pleasant to look at dressed as she was for exercise.

Late that morning, Tom was called to what was referred to as the Packing Shed to inspect the new equipment that had arrived earlier in the morning. He was greeted by Colonel Dubasso who showed him a special item he had arranged for Tom. It was a Marine Corps built 300 Winchester Magnum rifle built on a Winchester Model 70 action. It had a Zeiss scope mounted on it along with a laminated range data card for the five hundred custom loaded rounds of ammunition. There was a brand, new AK-47 with twenty new in the wrapper magazines along with two thousand rounds of ammunition.

In another hard case was a Mossberg 500 12-gauge shotgun with extra barrels. There were five hundred rounds of ammunition for the shotgun including one hundred and fifty rounds of 00 Buck shot and slugs then the rest in a mixture of Number 6 and 7 1/2 shot for hunting.

Even with the increased weight of weapons and ammunition, the launch weight was still down by over a thousand kilos once the rest of the crew kicked back on the amount of gold they were going to take with them. But it was now up to the engineers to figure out how to get it loaded. The personal equipment was going into the storage space beneath each hibernation pod, then the rest of the space was for personal items. It would not be until the equipment was in place that each person would know what they could take.

Dubasso showed Tom an unmarked box that when Tom opened it he had to smile, then closed it back up. Dubasso just winked and walked away while Tom picked up the box, tucked in under his arm and walked out of the building with it.

Tom went back to his office and locked the box in his office safe, then went to find Paul McCabe to find out how he was doing with his search of the mission software. He found him in a small office in the data processing center working at a sub-station.

Captain Youngerford was sitting in the office reading a magazine. Tom looked at McCabe and thought the man looked as if he had not slept since he started on this mission. Tom indicated for the Captain to step out of the office.

"Skipper, has McCabe slept at all?"

"Not that I know of Gunny. If it wasn't for Deanna, I doubt he would have eaten either. She brings him his meals then makes him eat. He told me earlier that he has found three anomalies that would not have been a problem other than maybe a goofy instrument readout down the road. He fixed those and moved on."

"Good. Now what are you doing here instead of one of the others?"

"Gunny, my real job starts in space, even if I am the Mission Commander. Chief Sharpe said Pritchard stopped by last night and got real upset when McCabe told him what he was doing. Pritchard tried to get him to shut down his search of the system and Paul told him he was following the orders of the Mission Security Officer and to take his complaints to you. Sharpe said Pritchard turned from a pissed off red to a pale white in seconds. Gunny, would you like to explain what the hell is going on?"

"Captain, I understand you have been up to the Morbius, so it is a real vehicle."

"Yeah very real. It's an ugly beast, but will do the job it was designed for."

"Alright then. I've gone over some of the cost estimates and there has been nearly thirty billion dollars on it alone, not counting the costs of lifting parts and pieces up to it. Why was I recruited by the Mission Flight Director instead of Pritchard and his committee? Why did someone try to kill me? And why was Pritchard so upset when I offered to pay for all the new equipment out of my own pocket, and then you and the others chipped in to deal with the expense?"

49

"Those are some very intriguing questions Gunny?"

"Yeah. It's like trying to work a mathematical formula with some of the variables missing. The answer is incomplete."

"What are you thinking Gunny?"

"I'm thinking in just over two weeks, we go into hibernation and once that occurs, we have zero control of events. If I cannot find the variables to make the formula balance, I may have to exercise Article Nine of the Mission Charter."

"Article Nine? Are you kidding me?"

"No Skipper I am not. I will not risk the lives of a single person on this mission unless I know there is no other avenue to follow. From the moment I examined our survival equipment, I have been wondering if someone does not wish for this mission to succeed. I also looked at the cost sheets on the junk we will have to toss once on the ground, and they tally out much higher than what we just received to replace them with."

"I must be missing something here. Care to expand on your thinking a bit more?"

"Okay figure it like this. The White House would like to shut NASA down and spend the money on feel good services that produce nothing but leeches on the treasury. Once we launch, about all that can be said is the mission is underway, but it gains nothing for NASA except for a few folks that will have to stay and monitor the mission until we get out of range to make any manner of communication between Morbius and ground control."

Tom paused as if thinking about his next comments.

"But if the Morbius blows up in a very spectacular manner within sight of Earth while folks are watching through telescopes, we become even greater heroes and the public just might clammer for another attempt at such a mission, even if the cost is so high."

"That's reaching Gunny, but it still makes sense in an odd way. Do you know that Pritchard was originally on the list to go on the mission?"

"Let me guess. He volunteered."

"Yes, and he is married."

"Well this gives me something else to consider. But I have an idea that might shake a few snakes out of the trees. Give me a couple of days, then we'll hold a closed crew meeting to discuss the thought rattling around in my head."

"Sure thing Gunny."

Tom went back to his office and just sat pondering the situation before him. He knew he was intelligent, but never considered himself as smart as his IQ tests said he was. Tom never worked puzzles because he found them boring in that he did them too quick to make them entertaining. But why him as Mission Security Officer? What did he actually bring to the table that made him the logical choice for the job?

He sat that problem aside and went back to work examining the ship's cargo manifest and working the numbers on the length of time they could survive before their first crops would come in for harvest, if the seeds they were taking would grow in a foreign environment. Then there were the animal embryos to consider. Like the humans on the journey, these animals were already in stasis and their module attached to the Morbius. There was a large cross-section of animals for food to grow in tanks once on the ground, then released into the environment to hopefully grow and multiply.

Tom worked until he nearly missed the evening meal at the Center's cafeteria before going to his apartment. He showered and was reading the tech manual on the terrain crawler he would be driving the next day at White Sands in a training mission. The crawler was identical to the one already loaded in one of the modules attached to the Morbius.

His reading was interrupted by three hard knocks on his door. Tom put the manual down and picked up his pistol and walked to the door. Looking out the privacy port, he saw Colonel Dubasso standing in the hallway. He opened the door keeping the pistol out of sight.

"Can I help you Colonel?"

Dubasso put his finger to his lips indicating for Tom to be quiet and held up a meter in his other hand. Tom stepped back from the door and the Colonel entered then moved around the apartment watching the meter. He even went into the kitchen area then Tom's bedroom and bathroom before returning to the living room.

"Okay the apartment is clean. Tom, I talked to Youngerford a while ago. You serious about executing Article Nine?"

"Colonel you hired me to insure the protection of the crew. Unless I can find some answers to a few questions, I'll damn well do it."

"What do you need?"

"I need a complete background on Pritchard including financials. Something is not right with that sucker and I just can't lay my finger on it. You know he tried to stop McCabe from checking the software for the Morbius. Now why would he want to stop Paul from double checking the software?"

"Yeah I was thinking that also when Youngerford told me about that situation. Alright, I'll make a couple phone calls and get something rolling on Pritchard. What else?"

"Look me in the eye and tell me the real reason you selected me for this mission?"

"Because I've had a bad feeling about this mission from day one. When I put the word out that we needed someone for this assignment, your name popped up along with a couple hundred men, but the one thing that stood out above everything else is you have a nasty habit of questioning things that seem good on the outside, then turn up broken once into the nuts and bolts of it. That's why you are always held back for promotion. You are not subservient to the system. I came to you because I am too close the system to see the whole picture and hoped you would."

"Alright Colonel, I'll buy that reasoning. Is that also why the little extra you had brought in today?"

"The box?"

"Yeah."

"If you have to use it to protect your crew do so, and I'll make sure it'll never be traced back to you."

"I'm not worried about that. But understand if I do go that route, it will only be to protect my crew."

"Yeah, that's another reason you were selected. I've made a few bad decisions in my life, but selecting you is not one of them. Watch your ass and keep at it. Anything else?"

"Not at the moment Colonel."

"Alright then. Here, keep this meter and check the apartment from time to time. I have another one."

Dubasso handed the bug detector to Tom.

"Where did you get this?"

Dubasso laughed.

"The Director of the Defense Intelligence Agency and I were classmates at the Academy."

"I'm not going to ask, but I bet he'll be getting a phone call before long just to see what the odds are for this year's Army/Navy Game?"

"Something like that Tom. Good night."

"Good night Colonel."

Tom went back to reading the tech manual knowing he had just set things in motion that held their own pace to the final destination. An hour later he decided bed needed him more and called it a night.

At eight the next morning he boarded a helicopter along with Chief Wallace Green and Chief Andrew Sharpe for White Sands to spend the day working with the equipment they would have to use to build a settlement on a new world.

Tom was amazed at the abilities of the solar powered crawler he would have to get around in. It also had a hydrogen powered engine which could get close to two hundred miles on a tank of hydrogen. There was a hydrogen fracking plant included in their cargo which would break down water into hydrogen to use in all their equipment and the solar capability was to back up the hydrogen engine.

They returned to the Space Center just before five in the evening and went to find Asami. She was in the infirmary working with a compact monitoring system she would be using both in space and on the planet. He asked her if she still wanted to go to dinner and she told him she would and to pick her up at seven.

When he collected her at her apartment she was wearing a light blue flowered summer dress with her shoulder length hair pulled back into a pony tail. Once he had her seated in this truck he asked her where she would like to eat.

"Tom this might sound strange, but I've heard several people talk about a place called Schlotzsky's. They make sandwiches, and everyone says they are great."

"They are Asami. I've eaten at them several times all over the country when I can find one. Schlotzsky's it is then."

Tom knew where the Schlotzsky's was located at near the Space Center. Asami asked him to order for them since he had eaten there before, and he ordered her a small original sandwich with sour cream potato chips and she took a small unsweetened tea. The sandwich was cut in half and she was barely through the first half when Tom noticed a tear in her eye.

"Asami, what's wrong?"

"This tastes so wonderful, and I just realized I'll never taste anything like this again."

"I'll tell you what I'll do. I'll have Colonel Dubasso get the recipes for all of the ingredients and once we get the new settlement up and running, I'll see about duplicating it for you."

"Are you serious?"

"Certainly. We'll get rich having the first sandwich shop on the planet."

Asami laughed.

When Tom helped her back into the truck she reached out and took his arm and pulled him to her, then put her hand to his face. He leaned in and they kissed for a short time before he made sure her door was closed. Neither spoke as they drove back to their apartment complex and they sat in his truck for several minutes exchanging kisses before she opened her door and got out without speaking.

Tom drove on down to his parking space and just considered tonight a success. She had told him all she wanted was a nice evening and conversation which they had plenty of both, even with her getting a bit emotional about leaving so much behind.

He was only wearing his trousers when there was a knock on his door and looking out the peep hole, he saw Asami standing in the hall. He opened the door to find her wearing a Jade Green dressing gown with multi-color embroidery on it like many he had seen in shops on Okinawa. Her hair was down and brushed out.

As she walked past him she spoke.

"I've changed my mind about you Thomas Jenkins."

As she entered his bedroom door, the dressing gown hit the floor revealing her nude body. Tom just closed and locked the door, then followed her into the bedroom finding her laid out on his bed. He took his trousers then boxers off, turned out the lights and joined her.

All That Glitters

Tom was awakened by loud banging on his apartment door and looked at the clock on the night stand. It was 2:37 in the morning and Asami was laying almost on top of him. When the next set of hard knocks on his door rang through the apartment, she stirred, slip off his chest and looked up.

"What's going on Tom?"

"Not sure, but stay in here."

Tom found his pants and put them on, then took his pistol from the nightstand before going into the living room. Looking out the peep hole he saw Paul McCabe standing there looking impatient and in a hurry. Tom opened the door.

"What's up Paul?"

"I found something. Let me in."

Tom stepped aside and let Paul in and watched as he was as antsy as an expectant father waiting for news of the birth of his first child.

"Alright Paul what did you find?"

"One hundred lines of code that is basically a self-destruct command. This is not unusual, but it was linked to a timer. Based on the simulation I ran on it, we would have been boosting past Mars when it was scheduled to blow. Tom, someone wants this mission to fail."

Tom heard a sound of someone lightly gasping and looked to see Asami standing in his bedroom door wrapped in a sheet. Paul turned to see Asami.

"Shit. Sorry Tom, I didn't realize you have company."

"It's alright Paul. Now back to the code. Any trace on it? About who might have put it in the system?"

"That's the good thing. When I first worked on the software, I put a few lines in that provides for date and time for any entry into the code in case we have to go back in and change something. No one can enter into the coding with a password, and each individual who has access to the code has their own password."

"Who wrote the destruction code?"

"Doctor Ronald Pritchard. He wrote the base line program for the mission where I did the fill out on it. There are four other engineers who have access, and their work is clean from everything I have seen so far."

"Paul, have you gotten any sleep at all?"

"Yeah, I've taken a nap here and there, but I still have a lot of code to look at. Maybe another twenty-four hours."

"Listen, can you save the bad program and reset the program without the destruct code?"

"Already done that. Look, I know you are worried about me not getting any rest, but this takes priority. I'm going to get a lot of rest once we go to sleep, but we won't wake up if there is anything else in the software. I'll find the problems, you take care of the source."

"Fine. Anyone else know about this?"

"Miguel is with me. He's out in the hallway waiting for me to head back to the lab."

"Alright, tell Miguel to keep this under his hat until we have more information. Do not discuss this with anyone without my approval. Understand?"

"Yeah, I understand."

"Paul, not even Deanna."

Paul gave him a questioning look, the nodded.

58

"Asami, you heard what I just said to Paul. This applies to you also."

"Yes Tom, I understand."

"Paul, you're doing good work. Stay at it, but try to get some rest when you can."

"I will Tom. I best get back to it."

After Paul left Tom walked over to Asami who was still standing in the door, picked her up and kissed her before carrying her back to bed. As he laid her down on the bed, she held onto him and whispered in his ear.

"Tom, make love to me again."

Tom lay in bed looking at the ceiling as Asami lay with her head on his shoulder considering what the past few hours had brought to his doorstep. He did not feel he had enough information to deal directly with Pritchard at this time, even with the programming codes linked to him, but he had to be dealt with, and in the next two weeks, otherwise he would shut down the program until things were fixed. He was still awake when the alarm went off at five.

When Tom got to his office at seven, the head of security for NASA was standing in the hallway outside his door.

"Can I help you Mister Mitchell?" Tom asked as he was unlocking his office door.

"Yes, Mister Jenkins, I think you can. Shall we go to my office and talk?"

"No. We'll talk in mine."

Tom entered his office and turned on the coffee maker that he had prepared before leaving the day before, then offered Mitchell a seat before sitting down behind his desk. The old rule was whoever was behind the desk, was in charge of the conversation, and Tom was not going to be put in the position of being on the wrong side of the desk.

"What's on your mind Mister Mitchell?"

"You have Paul McCabe in the Computer Lab running the Morbius mission code, and he has locked everyone out of the system while doing that. Doctor Pritchard has filed a complaint that without his access to the code, he cannot insure the safety of the mission. McCabe has informed me he is acting under your orders. Care to explain this?"

"Mister Mitchell, under Article Nine of the Mission Charter, I have the final and ultimate say so concerning the safety of the crew, and the mission. I have yet to hear any report on how a tank of Argon was tied into my oxygen feed lines at the pool which put me in the Infirmary. When I challenged the purchase of twenty-eight items we would be using for survival upon reaching our destination, there was an attempt to disallow any change in our equipment, until I offered to pay for it myself. Which I must say upset Doctor Pritchard. Now there are some other things I have discovered, but those I shall keep to myself until I can find a solid basis for making them public."

"Mister Jenkins, as head of security for NASA, I need to be in the loop concerning your actions here at the Space Center."

Tom leaned across his desk and looked hard at Mitchell.

"Mister Mitchell, until I am one hundred percent you are part of the solution, and not involved in the problem, I'll operate in the manner I have been operating. There is an attempt to sabotage this mission and I have no idea who all the players are at this time."

"Are you accusing me of being a part in a plan to sabotage the mission?"

"No. I'm saying I have no idea who all the players are, and I will not disclose, or discuss this with people I do not already trust.

This is the first conversation you and I have had between us since my arrival. Why is that?"

Mitchell just looked at Tom for a long time before answering.

"Doctor Pritchard informed me that I was not to have contact with you, so you could exercise your assignment without interference. He said he wanted to be able to observe your handling of things without my help."

"Don't you find that a bit odd considering he just ordered you to find out what I am up too concerning the mission codes?"

"Yes, now that I think about it, you're right it is odd. What can I do to earn your trust?"

"First of all, place a guard on the lab McCabe is using and only crew members, and Colonel Dubasso are authorized entrance until McCabe completes his assignment. And McCabe does not leave the lab without an escort. I don't know who all the players are in this, but if one of my crew gets hurt on the ground, it had better be by their own miscalculation during training."

"Based upon your own paranoia, don't you think one of my men could be involved?"

"I have considered that, and even have considered you might be involved, but I can guarantee that anyone involved will find what it is like inside Leavenworth if they are found out. I have taken steps to insure a microscope will be shoved up the ass of anyone that even looks like they are part of the problem. Call this a Dead Man's Switch if you will, but if anything happens that even smells of wrong doing, the switch is thrown, and no one can stop it until the final speck of dust falls to the grown. I might be just another stupid Marine, but I do know people in places you do not want to look into your activities. Do we have an understanding?"

Mitchell looked visibly shaken by Tom's last statement.

"Yes Mister Jenkins, we have an understanding."

Tom stood and offered his hand to Mitchell.

"I don't expect you to like me, or that we will become friends, but I have no problem with you calling me Tom as we work through this. I will ask you to keep this conversation as quiet as possible, even to Doctor Pritchard for now. Just in case the walls have ears."

Mitchell took Tom's hand.

"This is part of the trust issue, isn't it? Alright, you have a deal. Tom, my name is James."

"James, I hope our next meeting is on much friendlier terms."

"So do I Tom, so do I."

Tom watched Mitchell leave his office thinking he had just made the largest bluff in his life. But he considered that if Dubasso was going to get the information on Pritchard, he would consider doing it to anyone else if something bad happened to any of the crew.

All Tom could do now was go through the motions as he had tasks to complete and some more training. This wasn't the Marine Corps where everyone took for face value that the other guy in the uniform will do what he is supposed to do until proven otherwise. Here you had to assume everyone was the enemy until proven otherwise. Tom had to admit to himself he hated working with civilians that were ingrained in the civil service system because they would normally look out for themselves, before looking out for the person next to them.

The day seemed to drag by as Tom kept waiting for McCabe to finish his assignment and bring him the final results of the search. Asami had stopped by just before lunch and she reminded him she needed to eat. They ate in the cafeteria and just talked about their lives before NASA. She never brought up the events of the previous night, and never made any indication of following up on those activities anytime soon.

When Tom returned to his office McCabe was waiting for him along with a NASA security guard and Colonel Dunback, the Deputy Mission Commander.

"We got'em Tom. Pritchard is our saboteur."

"Paul are you positive? Are you sure there is no way he can claim someone hacked his password? We have zero margin of error here."

"The self-destruct data can be traced directly to Pritchard's office terminal. His office is key-coded and recorded so he would have to claim someone hacked his office then his terminal. No Tom he is dirty."

"What are you going to do now Gunny?" Colonel Dunback asked.

"I am going to do nothing at the moment. Colonel Dunback, gather up the crew and request to see the gold we were going to take up with us, so each member can determine how much weight they wish to use on gold. I've already stated how much I will take, but the rest of you are having trouble making that decision. The gold is supposed to on site and locked in one of the vaults. I'm wondering how much is gold or just gold-plated lead?"

"Oh, shit Gunny. Are you saying Pritchard is doing this for profit?" Dunback inquired.

"That's one scenario I'm considering. Get on it, and put the Chiefs on that vault in case someone tries to move the gold before we can examine it."

"I'll add a female or two to that watch list just in case someone wants to get rough. They might not wish to assault a female."

"Use your best judgement Colonel. Paul, damn good work. Now I need you to stay up and about for a while longer, but once finished, get to bed as early as possible and get your rest."

"No problem Tom. No argument from me."

Less than thirty minutes later Tom stood in the shadows of the main office building as he watched Pritchard nearly run to his car and left in a hurry. He smiled, then headed for the vault containing the gold, knowing his crew would be there by now. Tom had the overall weight of all the gold for the crew on a copy of the manifest before his change, and the estimated weight of the gold if already sold to pay for the new equipment.

A scale was brought in and checked for calibration, then they began weighing the gold. Michael Lathrop, the crew's Geologist took charge of the weighing and insured each number of gold coins were on the scale at each weighing to insure there was no switching of gold for gold plated metal. Tom estimated it would take roughly one hundred and seventeen pounds of gold to pay for the new equipment. Fifty-three kilos was the limit of any missing gold.

When the scale began to give readings outside the possible deviation of the weight per coin count, the rest of the crew began to scratch the metal of every coin in the count to determine if plated, or just short on weight. Lead began to surface beneath some of the coins meaning they were plated, and other than the gold used in the plating, they were worthless.

James Mitchell had come to observe the process and when the lead coins began to crop up, he just looked at Tom then ordered that Pritchard be located, and returned to the Space Center based upon the entry logs of the vault kept by the Security Office. Pritchard had been inside the vault several times, and it appeared he was exchanging fake coins for real ones. His removal of gold to pay for the new equipment was listed and when accounting for the fake coins, there was over one hundred kilos of gold missing from the vault.

Three hours later, Doctor Ronald Pritchard was located in his car at the bottom of Galveston Bay, after he had driven his car off a dock, drowning himself rather than face justice.   It would be a week before the DIA investigation exposed the reasons for Pritchard's activities. He was heavily in debt, and even having married a woman with a large trust fund, he had no access to that money and was being pressured to pay up on his debts. His own desire to be part of the mission was in part to skip out on those debts since some were gambling debts.

In Pritchard's wallet were the names of four NASA employees that he was paying to cause problems for the mission. Those people were quietly removed from employment and were told if they filed any grievance, they would stand before a judge concerning their activities in the pay of Pritchard.

It was speculated that Pritchard had been skimming off the gold long before Tom arrived, but when he offered to cash out instead of taking the gold with him, that gave way to the knowledge that not all the gold was in fact gold.

The only thing that made sense concerning the self-destruct coding in the software was that Pritchard was jealous of the fact he had been refused membership on the crew, even though he had two shuttle missions under his belt.

Asami did not come to Tom's apartment that night, but returned the next night, and spent every night they had left on Planet Earth with him.

The night before the crew was to go into hibernation, they held a party remembering that they had to refrain from alcohol that night, but enjoyed an evening of good food and music with couples dancing until late. That night every man took a woman to their bed as this was the last night they may ever see, and no one wanted to spend it alone. Tom and Asami exhausted themselves.

Departure

Tom stood back as each of the crew were put into their pods and the hibernation process began. He shook Colonel Dubasso's hand, then entered his pod and closed his eyes as the technicians hooked him into the system. He felt a cold rush through his body then total darkness as he went to sleep.

The crew were going to be lifted in two lifts with six males, and six females per lift. Tom was not on the same lift as Asami, but once asleep that was of no concern. He was in the first lift which went off on schedule, but the second lift was delayed twelve hours due to weather. The remote attachment of both pods went according to plan, then a thirty-day countdown began as the systems were being checked, and rechecked.

The initial boost went smoothly utilizing the same solid fuel rockets that lifted the space shuttle into orbit. The rockets were ejected thirty seconds after the on-board computers recognized complete burn on the rockets, and secondary rockets pushed them away from the vehicle to just end up drifting in space.

A week later, the Hyper-jet engines fired off sending the vehicle towards its final objective. The on-board computers ran hourly checks of the vehicle and crew, sending that data back towards Earth as it also received news updates concerning what was happening on Planet Earth for the crew to review later.

Two months after launching, the radio signals from the Morbius were coming in broken and with static. This told the ground crew it was far enough away that it had completely left the solar system and was on a free trajectory to its final goal.

Time passed on Planet Earth as the Morbius silently flew through space as the shielding in place to protect the different modules were slowly becoming worn away as micrometeorites impacted them. It was estimated the shielding would last to their estimated target planet.

When the sitting President learned of the Morbius mission, he did everything he could to reduce NASA's budget and retire the space shuttles. Two President's later the shuttles were finally retired, and once again NASA was having to rely of other methods of going into space.

Thirty years after the launching of Morbius the public was told of the expedition and the crew became overnight heroes. Twenty years later a second, much larger vehicle, was launched with over seven hundred crew members. Years of calculations went into determining the path of Morbius before the Prometheus was launched.

No one knew what they would find if they did locate the Morbius, but humanity has always flown on hope. A decade later humanity nearly came to a fiery end with another World War, with armies using nuclear weapons on the battlefield.

Book Two

A New World to Conquer

Long range sensors finally detected a planet which fit the criteria for establishing a settlement. Eighty percent of the planet was covered by water, and from long range sensor data had a near earth like mixture within its atmosphere to support human life.

As the Morbius entered the planets solar system, it launched a pair of sensor pods towards the planet. If their readings did not fall within the boundary of what would be considered an inhabitable planet, the Morbius would fly on by, looking for another planet in another solar system to take up orbit around.

The readings came back close to the mean data required for life when compared to earth. As the Morbius moved into orbit over the planet, the life support computers began to slowly awaken its passengers. In doing so it activated specific elements of their hibernation suits to massage the leg and arm muscles to elevate the stiffness within the muscle from eons of hibernation. At the same time the modules containing human cargo began to vent out the inert gases which had protected the interior from the effects of oxygen over the eons of flight, and replaced them with a mixture of Nitrogen and Oxygen much like the air of Planet Earth.

They were in orbit almost a month before the first pods began to open exposing its human cargo to the atmosphere. Captain Youngerford, Patrice Grant who was the crews Environmental Engineer, Tom, then Paul McCabe were the first awakened. Even though their bodies had been fed nutrients as they were coming awake, and the electrodes had massaged their limbs, they were stiff and were slow in moving.

An hour later Doctor James Ostrow, MD was awakened along with Karen Costello. Once they were able to move around, they removed the catheters and other items plugged into the other's bodies, then took turns removing their own. Even before they dealt with the growth of hair on their bodies while asleep, Youngerford and Tom began looking at the data being sent up from the surface of the planet from the two probes already there.

While that was happening, Paul McCabe was running a complete systems check to insure they didn't open a hatch to the vacuum of space. Patrice Grant was examining the readouts from each module to determine if they were stabilizing to near earth normal. All of this was being done remotely in their module and not from the command deck until they were ready to move to that location.

The rotation of the planet below them was determined to be twenty-three hours and eighteen minutes long. Gravity was computed to be .93 that of Earth. The air below was calculated to be .02 percent richer in Oxygen than Earth, and the other inert elements in the atmosphere were close to Earth normal.

They found a location in what they considered the Northern Hemisphere of the planet with what appeared to be an Inland Sea with large open planes stretching for miles, before becoming thickly forested. Tom asked Youngerford to send a survey crawler to a location near the sea, so they could get a sample of the water and such. What looked like grass was pinker than green, and it would be nice to know that it was not dangerous to place a foot onto due to acids or other poisons within the plant structure.

The survey crawler they sent down was of the same classification of those sent to Mars to explore the Red Planet. The Morbius had six of these small vehicles to test the earth of the planet they were orbiting. In the backs of everyone's minds was the fact that unless the initial probes failed in their mission, they were at the end of their journey.

If the probes had failed, then they were stuck in orbit until they used up all supplies, and oxygen could no longer be scrubbed to provide them with a breathable atmosphere. All they could do was hope that the probes were accurate and below them was a new life.

The location for setting the survey crawler probe down was figured and set into the computer. On the next orbit it would launch so it would land in proximity to the chosen site. A circuit test of the launch vehicle and the crawler showed the electronics had survived the trip, but one critical aspect would not be known until the drop. Did the material in the parachute survive? This was extremely important since all the modules which would drop to the planet, had parachutes which were made from the same exotic material.

There was no way to watch the actual drop, but the readouts from the drop vehicle stayed inside perimeters for the drop. The parachute material had survived the years in an atmosphere of inert gases. All they could do was wait until the vehicle opened and allowed the crawler to accomplish its mission. After that, all that was left to do was to get cleaned up, and wake up the rest of the crew.

The schedule for waking everyone up was set at four people at a time once the initial group was up. Asami was in the second group, and the first of her module to be awaken, so she could help with any medical problems that may arise. Everyone looked good according to the read-outs until an hour before he was to be awaken, Roger Lindstrom, the crew's mechanical engineer began to show signs of heart failure. Asami and Doctor Ostrow work feverishly to keep him within the baseline norms, but he died within minutes of awakening. They sealed him back into his pod and just moved on, taking care of those who had made the trip.

The original projection for the mission was the possibility of losing ten percent of the crew due to a variety of situations and problems which were unpredictable. Captain Youngerford decided that Lindstrom would be buried on the planet below instead of his pod being jettisoned into space as tribute to him. The effect on the crew would not be noticeable until after they were on the ground as they were all just happy to still be alive.

Once the crew was up, cleaned up and ready, they met in the command module for a briefing. It was cramped in the module, but they could all see the main monitor showing the planet below them. Youngerford started the briefing.

"Well folks here we are and so far, it looks like we have a new home. Now for the real interesting part. According to the computer, today's date is March 22nd, 8337. Where we are at in the universe is still unknown, but our primary antenna is functional and pointed as close as the computer can figure towards where Earth might be, and a signal is going out to let Earth know we made it. I can only hope there is someone back there listening."

Tom took over the brief.

"So far it appears the Morbius survived with minor damage and we'll be able to drop each module without a problem. But we will not open a passageway to the other modules without sealing the areas we know are safe, then opening the next area to persons wearing hard suits, just in case there is a leak that has not been detected, or has not been properly ventilated. I'll assign teams to check each module once everyone has a chance to become fully awake and the stiffness out of the joints. Right now, I feel every one of those years on the computer."

That got a small laugh from the crew.

"Now we have sent down a survey crawler to check our proposed landing site, and so far, the data looks good. You'll notice that the color of the grass is different, but tests on it shows to very similar to earth grass with a bit more protein in it. Once we can get our cattle out of their test tubes onto this grass, they should grow big and strong, giving us plenty of meat per hoof."

"Gunny, is there any indication of life down there?" Robert Grey asked. He was the crews Veterinarian.

"None yet Doctor Grey. But we are only surveying a small area right now. My first concern is the body of water near the landing site. Is it fresh water or salt water? Is it safe to drink or will something in it destroy our filtering systems, and make it dangerous to our systems? There are a lot of questions we need to have answered before we go down there. We can survive up here for a year before we have two choices to make. I'm not a big fan of the second choice."

Everyone knew what the second choice was, and no one wished to join Lindstrom in the afterlife.

As details were assigned, the crew went to work insuring if, and when they dropped, everything was ready to go. Asami found a moment to talk to Tom.

"Tom, I know it seems like just a couple days ago we were in your apartment, but if you decide that you want to explore the others, I understand."

"Asami, first it's too soon after waking up to even consider partners, but if I was going to explore the others, we would not have spent so much time together. I'm happy with what we have if you are."

"Yes Tom, I'm happy. And I'm very happy we both made it."

Over the next week, they dropped two more survey crawlers in other locations near the first one to get a feel of the area. One was dropped near the forest line and ventured into it to find out what might lurk in it.

Tom did two EVA's checking the exterior of the modules to insure they were sound, and did one repair on the ceramic tiles for reentry. Other crew members did EVA's for various reasons in preparation to drop to the planet once Tom felt they had enough information to risk the drop.

In his own mind he knew he would rather die with his feet firmly planted on solid ground instead of in the vacuum of space, but he was still not going to risk anyone's lives based on his own feelings.

The crawlers were detecting insect life, but until on the ground, they could not determine if they would put a human at risk, or if they were just bugs. The crawler that went into the forest was picking up movement of large animals, but could never get a clear photo of one, only shadows moving just out of camera range.

During one crew meeting it was suggested that the photos were taking pictures of intelligent creatures since a normal, earth based creature would approach the crawler to determine if it was dangerous to them, as ground tests on earth had shown in several locations.

Regardless of the time of day, there was never detected smoke or infrared photos of living creatures within the region. This posed a question whether any creatures on the planet could be cold blooded.

Two weeks after the last person had come out of hibernation, the crew was ready to drop. The only information they could not develop was if there was animal life in the inland, fresh water sea. This was something they would have to develop once on the ground. It was hoped that fish like animals would be available to add protein to their diet as they built a settlement.

Tom gave the go ahead for the drop. The weather in the drop zone was mild, and not knowing the weather patterns of the planet, he felt it was best to get down now and begin the building of the settlement.

The Drop

There were twenty-six modules counting the crew modules that needed to be dropped in to as small an area as possible. Each module was fifty feet long, and as big inside as a semi-trailer. Each module had been carefully loaded to balance the loads for lifting into space, then returning to earth. But the unique aspect of the modules was that once under their large parachute canopies, the lower, heat resistant hull would be blown away exposing caterpillar tracks so they could be moved utilizing electric motors powered by solar panels and small hydrogen motors to generate electricity.

Once on the ground and moved by hand held remote controls, the modules could extend stabilizers to level them. The crew modules were a different beast since the crew pods lined the interior of the module meaning some of the crew would find themselves facing down once they were on the ground making it the responsibility of those on the 'floor' to assist them from exiting their pods.

One last aspect of the modules were retro-rockets which would only ignite if the air speed of the module was too fast for a safe landing. Each circuit was checked, then rechecked to ensure that everything was ready for the drop. One circuit on an equipment module had to be repaired before it gave a green light during a test. They ran that circuit three more times to insure it was ready for the drop.

Using the first survey crawler's base platform as ground zero, Paul McCabe programmed the drops in a tight pattern near the base. He ran several simulations to check his programming before he ran one final simulation for Captain Youngerford, Colonel Dunback and Tom. The parachute guidance system for each module would lock onto the signal from the crawler base, and offset it's decent according to the program if everything went as planned.

This was the one part no one had control of and everyone quietly feared. There was no place on the Morbius for a couple to be alone as they waited for the time to drop. Tom gave Asami a kiss, helped her with her helmet, then helped her into her pod before he closed it up for her. The pods were designed to survive an impact twice what was anticipated utilizing a foam like material which would filled the pod moments before impact, if the on-board computer read the modules air speed greater than designed.

Each pod had its own air supply and the individual would be wearing a helmet with face shield to prevent the foam from closing their mouths or noses preventing them from breathing. The foam would slowly dissolve over an hour after filling the pod leaving a messy, gooey residue that could be washed off without much effort.

Tom climbed into his pod and situated himself for the drop. Protocol for the drops required everyone to be in their pods even though the life support modules would be the last to drop. If anything went wrong during the drops, the computer could release all modules at the same time to prevent them from being caught up in damage with the primary vehicle.

The problem for the human cargo was they had to wait as only two modules were being dropped per orbit. This meant they could feel the modules before them kick off the Morbius as the computer announced each drop. The drops were scheduled to happen in which the life support modules would land just after midday.

All a person could do was lie in their pod and think. They had a small amount of water they could sip from a tube, and each person was wearing an adult diaper in case of need. Each pod was equipped with the ability to play music, or even an audio book to help with the long hours of waiting for their turn to drop.

Tom wished they could communicate with others in their pods to help calm any nerves that were becoming frayed, as his own were becoming stretched to the limit. Even though the computer alerted them ahead of time they were about to drop, it came as a surprise to everyone. Tom was lucky not to have communications with the other pods, as several of the pods were ringing with the screams of fear from both male and female.

The ride down was nerve racking for the crew as they first had to endure the buffeting of the module entering the atmosphere while strapped inside their pods. Next came a sudden stillness as the module entered the atmosphere, then the light jolt of the drogue chutes opening to slow down their decent. Then came the hard jolt as the six massive parachutes opened to begin their slow descent to the planet's surface.

Everyone was counting down the seconds knowing the panels hiding the tractor portion of the module would blow off which would tell them they were at approximately two thousand feet from the surface, if the small module's ground search radar was doing its job.

The noise and jolt of the panels blowing was greater than anyone imagined as they blew off, clearing the tractor element for landing. Everyone was holding their breaths as they waited to feel the emergency retro rockets fire to make for a soft landing, but neither life support module ignited their rockets as the modules gently impacted the surface.

A green light within the pods told the crew they were on the ground, and it was safe to exit their pods. Tom was in position in the module to exit without assistance, and immediately went to the assistance of the pod above him to help Karen Costello out of her pod.

Tom had one set rule for landing and that was no one was to exit their module until he had set foot on the planet, and was certain it was safe for everyone else, even though each person was to be armed until told otherwise. He had loaded all his magazines for his weapons during preparations to drop, and all he had to do was remove them, and his survival vest from the storage space beneath his pod.

He checked communications to the other module via his personal radio before he cracked the seal on the hatch leading to the outside world. Captain Youngerford was at his work station viewing the surrounding terrain via a remote camera atop the module. He could see all the other modules, and from his view point, they all seemed to have landed in proper order.

One final sensor reading of the surrounding atmosphere advising that the air was breathable, and no toxic fumes were developing around the module from entry. Tom cracked the seal to the module as everyone in the module stood back and watched. As the hatch opened, a small set of steps extended from under the hatch to the ground. Tom stepped out on the first step and looked around, then looked back into the module.

"Captain Youngerford. You're the mission Commander. Sir, take the first step onto our new world."

Youngerford looked at Tom, then nodded as he moved to the steps and moved by Tom. He paused, took a deep breath, then moved to the bottom step. He looked back up at Tom and those that could see out the hatch.

"I'm at a loss for words?

"Captain, I don't have any words either. Maybe no words are what we need."

Youngerford nodded and stepped off to become the first Morbius crewman to set foot on an alien planet. He walked out through the knee-high grass about twenty feet and looked around, then up at the sky before looking back at Tom.

"Tom, let's build a home."

Tom keyed his radio and told the second module to open-up and join the party. Four minutes later Asami was wrapped around his neck giving him a deep, passionate kiss.

Building a Settlement

The first priority was to erect shelters, which meant moving the modules from their landing positions closer to where the settlement would stand. There was a high point approximately five hundred meters further away from the inland sea which was determined as the best location for the actual settlement. It took nearly an hour to move the modules containing the pre-fab shelters into location from where they landed.

As the modules were being moved, Chief Green opened the first equipment module on location, and with the help of Chief Sharpe, assembled one of the mini-tractors and attached the bush cutter to it for clearing the high grass from the construction site.

Everyone had assignments to deal with as one by one the fourteen-foot, by twenty-foot aluminum reinforced fiberglass shelters were assembled. Asami and Doctor Ostrow had opened the medical module and were inspecting the birth control implants stored within to insure they were still capable of preforming as prescribed, then they removed the old ones and inserted new ones into the females of the crew. It had been determined that the first year the settlement should not risk a female becoming pregnant until the settlement was firmly established, and the crew had paired up.

In the back of everyone's mind was the reality that now there was one more female who would not have a mate because of Roger Lindstrom's death. Of the crew that had already somewhat paired up in Houston, Lindstrom was not one of them.

Every person was trained to move a module and had trained on shelter assembly during their yearlong training at Houston and other locations, which allowed the other modules to be moved while others were erecting shelters. Four people could erect a shelter in just under two hours and Youngerford assigned four crews to do that assembly, while others moved the modules closer to the build site.

Youngerford also insisted that Tom refrain from assisting since he was responsible for security, and even though the survey crawlers had not detected any dangerous life forms or large animals, Youngerford felt it was best he stay alert and watch for anything the crawlers had missed.

Once the modules were in position the individuals moving them jumped in to assist in assembling the shelters. All that was being accomplished at this point was the basic shelters. Water supply, sanitation, and other aspects of the shelters would be fitted once the shelters were up and could be used that night to replace the pods in the crew modules, especially since half of the pods were upside down now.

Four tent type porta-johns had been set up to be used by the crew to remove bodily waste while building the shelters. A pit was dug for the waste to be buried nightly until other arrangements could be made for its disposal. It was noticed that the time in orbit had slightly weakened the bodies, but no one slacked off from the effort to get the job done. Meal breaks occurred as a single individual would take a short period to consume a ration, then get back to work as the next individual took their break, giving a continuous construction activity at the site.

Tom had positioned himself atop one of the modules, so he could obtain an unobstructed view of the settlement site, and the surrounding terrain. As this was being taken care of, the two Navy Seabee's were busy digging a large hole to drive two of the modules into later, which would serve as septic tanks for the waste from the shelters, once that module was empty of its cargo of shelter components. They were positioned in tandem, then lateral lines were laid to allow the waste water to filter out through the soil. Once in position, the solar/hydrogen powered motors would be removed along with other parts of the power train system for use at another time.

By sunset, there were eight shelters up and ready to provide protection for the night. It was decided by the crew under the suggestion of Captain Youngerford that everyone just bed down and in the shelters with six people occupying the command module to watch the ground radar for intrusion along with the infrared cameras during the night. Tom would be one of the individuals in the command module, so he could react quickly from that site instead of having to be located and informed of a possible problem.

The night was quiet and in the morning the crew gathered to eat the morning rations while discussing the day's work schedule. Water samples were to be taken and tested from the inland sea, even though the survey crawler had determined it was fresh water and free from harmful chemicals or bacteria.

The SeaBee's were to attach the small entrencher and dig a trench down to the sea where they would lay a four-inch Kevlar, reinforced hose to draw water to the settlement. One of the side benefits to the foam that was to be used in the pods during a hard landing, was that when additional chemicals were added, it set up like concrete and had been tested in several environments on Earth showing it was extremely durable, and did not require the metal reinforcement concrete required.

A water purification unit would need to be set up between the sea and the settlement to insure the water would be safe for drinking on such a pad. The unit was solar powered with the addition of the drive motor from a module. There was a fracking unit with the water purification unit which would pull water from the purified side of the unit, frack it to gain the hydrogen, and run the motor which in turn would provide power to the water purification unit as needed.

It would take a week, seven days before the shelters were complete, sanitation installed and the water supply set into place before the shelters were finished. Solar panels atop each shelter provided base power to each shelter until a larger power station could be constructed and tied into each shelter.

The second module containing the shelters and their appliances was moved to higher ground, stripped of everything inside, checked for cracks in its polymer coated lining then elevated as high as it's jacks would allow then sealed. The primary water line was attached, and it became the water storage tank for the settlement. A primary line was laid from it to a junction point at the settlement, so water could be supplied to the shelters.

This was one thing that NASA had over planned for and it worked out perfectly as they had left over water and sewage line once everything was in place.

Those couples that had already paired up finally were able to spend their first night together as lovers in their new homes. The others took to the shelters either as two men or two women sharing a shelter until they paired up.

In the shelter, or home that Tom shared with Asami that first night was a link to the ground radar which would alert him if anything was detected by it.

The biological clock of the crew said they had left Houston just short of two months considering the time they spent in orbit, even if the clock said it had been over six millennia.

How the time and distance from Earth would affect the crew was undetermined, nor could it be predicted. There was still much to do and knowing that their individual survival depended on the support of one another was a key factor in the work they had done, and the work that lay ahead.

The Wedding

They had been on the ground a month setting, then resetting the left-over modules, to provide easy access to medical and laboratory facilities as the ground near was cleared, plowed and their first crops were planted. The ground was rich in nutrients which should provide them with fresh vegetables within a couple of months while the embryos of cattle and other meat providing animals were being thawed out and grown in the labs.

NASA had planned rations for four years and each shelter had a week's supply of ration packs issued and logged to keep track of their supplies. These were dehydrated rations, but once infused with hot water and the included spices added, they were tasty, if not gourmet meals. The powdered drinks gave some relief to the blandness of drinking purified water and the crew settled into a daily regime of work building a sustainable life.

Prior to the drop, they had launched six weather satellites into orbit above the continent where the settlement was located, in order to help predict the weather and its patterns. Once the command module was firmly set into place and the pods removed, Mia Lathan, their Meteorologists set up her equipment in it to keep an eye on the weather, along with other instruments set atop the module.

In many ways NASA had overdone much of what had been planned for in that there were often three sets of equipment spread out in various modules in case they lost a module during the trip or drop. There were even three commercial sewing machines available so that the large parachutes could be cut up, and resewn into usable packs, bags or other items.

When the one-hundred-foot communications antenna was erected, one of the parachutes was attached to it with the antenna going through the open center of the parachute, and a pad was formed beneath it as a gathering place for the crew. Tables and benches were constructed from the blow off panels from the modules that they could locate and gather up once the main work of establishing the settlement was complete.

The first meeting under the canopy was held and a name for their new colony was voted on. The settlement and planet would be referred to as Lindstrom, after Roger Lindstrom who was now buried in his pod at the edge of the settlement. The pods which had been removed from the modules were being stored in another module to be used as caskets, if, and when needed. A reminder that life was fragile, and often short.

Regardless of their education and training, once the settlement was firmly established, each member became farmers to insure the settlement survived. Other skills had been learned at Houston, and again in the first days on Lindstrom. It was discovered that if a thin slice of the padding from the pods was used along with material from a parachute, soft, comfortable moccasins could be made which were found to be extremely light and durable.

It seemed that everyone had tasks to deal with as they assisted in the labs, even if not their main function. All except for Tom. His life revolved around moving from point to point on the grassy plain they were set upon to the inland sea searching for anything that might be a danger to them. But the one place he had not ventured into was the forest, six kilometers from the settlement.

Slowly the crew began to pair up with the females often moving from male to male determining who they wanted to spend the rest of their lives with. Everyone took the movement of the unattached females as a natural occurrence and there were no hard feelings if one moved on. Deanna Howell kept a log of the daily goings on and never mentioned a name of who was sleeping with who any given night, and often found herself sitting under the canopy talking to a male or female about their concerns.

Unknown to the men, the females had determined amongst themselves that since they were now a male short, if the single female wished to mate with a male for the purpose of bringing forth a child, the mated females would allow her to mate with the male of their choice, and even support the activity to gain another member of the settlement. This would later cause some laughter and minor problems for the males, but they even would understand the reasons for it.

Asami noticed that when Tom was upon the watch platform built above the command module, he spent most of his time looking towards the forest. She knew he was going to explore it sooner or later, and there would be nothing she could do to stop him. She finally approached the subject one evening during a crew get-together.

"Tom, you're going to explore the forest, aren't you?"

"Yes Asami, I am. It needs to be done for our own protection."

"Are you going alone, or taking someone with you?"

"Alone. My sole function is security, while everyone else has a solid purpose. I'll not risk another's life in there, only my own."

The crew was silent as they listened to Tom and Asami discuss his plan.

"Thomas Jenkins, before you do, we will make our mating legal and permanent, and you will leave me with a child."

"Honey, I have no problem with marrying you, but it was agreed upon to wait until we have been here at least a year before bringing new life to this world."

"Yes, but none of the other men will be going off into the unknown, maybe to never return. Give me a child, or we end our relationship now."

Asami had never made a single demand upon Tom and he knew the reason she was making such a demand. They both loved each other even if the words were never spoken. Tom looked around the gathering at the faces of the others, then looked back at Asami. Captain Youngerford spoke before Tom had a chance.

"Master Gunnery Sergeant Jenkins. I'm not sure if I am speaking for the crew, but if not for you we'd be space dust orbiting Mars. The fact that you do not wish a traveling companion to go with you into the forest speaks of your concern for the crew, so I will say this. If you are intent on marrying Doctor Nakajima and she expects to carry your child while you are gone on a walk about of the forest, then she will get her wish as an exemption to the rules we decided before leaving Earth. Any objections from the crew?"

The only sounds made were those of agreement with the Captain's statement.

Tom looked around and saw the crew nodding their approval.

"I can't fight all of you and will not fight you, Asami. If that is what you wish, then you shall have it. It will delay my trip, but I can live with that."

"Tom, it'll take a few days before the effects of the implant are out of my system, then it will all depend on nature. I'll have James remove mine this evening."

"Whatever you want Asami. Are we going to have a wedding ceremony, or just call it what it is between us?"

"Captain Youngerford?"

"Asami, this was never covered at Houston. If we want to consider this planet as my ship, then I can and will marry you both. But then again, who is going to challenge the two of you stating before the crew that you are now joined by marriage?" Youngerford responded.

Asami looked at Tom.

"Thomas Jenkins, are you my husband from this day forward?"

"I am Asami Nakajima. Are you my wife from this day forward?"

"I am Thomas."

"Do you wish to keep your maiden name or accept mine from this day forward?"

"From this day forward let the records of the Planet Lindstrom show my name as Asami Jenkins."

Tom looked at Deanna Howell.

"Deanna, since you are keeping a log of events, please notate in that log this date as the joining of myself and Asami Nakajima as a wedded couple."

"I shall Tom. It will be logged as the Earth Date according to the computer and the planet date as of our arrival."

"Well kiss the bride ya dumb Jarhead!" Chief Green hollered from the crowd.

Tom laughed as he picked Asami up and she wrapped her arms around his neck. The kiss was long and received a lot of cat calls from the crew until she broke the kiss, and told him to put her down so they could remove her implant.

When she returned after her implant had been removed, a small party was held celebrating the wedding. As the party broke up, couples paired up for the evening with Jayne Martin, their Dentist, begging off since she was having her period at that time.

Asami was vigorous in bed that night and in the privacy of their small home exchanged the words of love to each other. Tom went to sleep considering how short of time they had known each other, but he felt comfortable with Asami, and she seemed content with him. He fell asleep thinking he could not remember Joanna's face.

Time passed with Asami getting her period four days after their wedding while Tom prepared for his exploration of the forest. Mia Lathan configured the weather satellites to detect the tracking device in Tom's communications unit. The weather satellites were slowly developing a mapping of the terrain, but Tom felt comfortable with knowing which direction he was heading, since from space, they thought the inland sea was to the north of the plain where they set up the settlement, but once on the ground, Tom's old military compass said the sea was to the east of the settlement.

Tom gave Chief Sharpe three gold coins and asked him to fashion wedding bands from them. It took the Chief two days to work the coins into wedding rings, and the exchange of rings took place in the common area at the evening meal. Three weeks after Tom and Asami married she was pregnant.

Into the Unknown

Three days after it was confirmed that Asami was expecting their child, they said their goodbyes just at daylight under the canopy with the crew in attendance. Chief Green was going to take Tom to the edge of the forest with a tractor crawler, so he would not have to walk the distance.

Tom never looked back as he carefully moved into the forest and through the thick underbrush at the edge of the forest. The survey crawler that had ventured into the forest showed once past the initial underbrush the terrain beneath the forest canopy thinned out, but it was those first meters that death could suddenly rear its head, since vision was down to mere feet instead of meters.

It had been considered to send a survey crawler along to help transport supplies such as additional water, but its range was limited due to the inability to recharge via its solar panels due to the overlapping canopy of the forest, and Tom knew he had to go deep into the forest to learn about it.

He carried two weeks' worth of rations broken down to conserve the bulk space along with four liters of water. In his pack was a water purification kit to filter out any micros and such from pools of water he might find to supplement what he was carrying. He also had a test kit for any fruit, or what might be edible plants found inside the forest to determine if they contained any harmful chemicals or minerals.

Tom was carrying an AK-47 with a sound suppressor on it as his primary manner of protection plus his old 1911 pistol. He had packed, then repacked his field pack five times before he found the load he wanted to carry on this trip. His shelter was a two-person survival tent that had to be strung between trees and he had cut the shroud lines from a parachute giving him four lengths of Kevlar reinforced line in lengths sixty feet long.

There was also a small, hand crank charger to recharge any battery he might need, even though he was carrying two spares of each type battery for his radio and other systems including lights.

He took his time as he passed through the underbrush into the thinner vegetation looking for any signs of animal activity. No worn paths which animals often use as they move in and out of an area could be found. Tom could hear sounds that might be caused by insects, but the lack of noise was almost unsettling. He checked his back trail from time to time just in case something decided to track him and make a meal out of him.

Even the light tracks of the survey crawler had been erased by nature so Tom had nothing to compare his own path too. He took breaks from time to time to just listen for any sounds that might indicate life of any type other than the insects they had already discovered.

Every two hours his radio would beep twice, and he would break squelch once letting the settlement know he was still alive and safe. He was not concerned about his compass bearing since once he decided to return to the settlement, he would ask for a compass bearing based upon his location fixed by a satellite for his return trip. Tom thought it was a waste of time for the settlement to beep him since they could watch his movement as a blip from the satellites, but he knew that it would make life for Asami easier.

Tom kept a careful eye on his watch as he did not want to be caught too close to nightfall and have to set a camp in the dark. He had done this all over the world, and knew in forest canopy as he was under, night came quick, and would catch a person off guard if not prepared for it.

When he decided to make camp, he called back to the settlement to advise them he was stopping for the night. As soon as he had his tent erected, he took a small, folding wire stool from his pack and sat on it instead of the ground as he ate a light meal. He tossed a bit of his ration onto the leaf covered ground out in front of him and watched as after a few minutes, bugs came from under the leaves to attack the unknown food source. A couple of bugs went to it then moved away, while others covered and even seemed to fight over the morsel of food.

It bothered Tom that a planet had an abundance of insect life yet no animal life other than the fish they had found near the inland sea shoreline. Nadal Konoval, their Biologist, was in the process of constructing a gill net from shroud lines to harvest fish for consummation once tested for edibility.

As darkness fell, Tom could swear he saw movement out of the corner of his eye, but never could get a fix on anything moving within the forest. Tom put on his night vision goggles and continued to scan the terrain around him, looking for anything that might indicate animal life. Something was out there, but he could never get a fix on it.

Tom stayed out of his tent until he knew he had to remove the goggles to prevent his eyes from becoming strained from their overuse. He had cleared out the leaves from in front of his tent and checked to see if any bugs were at the opening before he unzipped it, brushed off his trousers and boots and crawled inside.

He radioed the settlement that he was going to sleep and was turning off his radio for the night. Tom lay on his lightweight sleeping bag listening to the night around him and from time to time it seemed he could hear a rustling of leaves, but nothing that sounded threatening. There was only two times he could go to sleep on his back. One was when in the field and the other when a lover was on his shoulder after making love. He gave up and let sleep take him.

The next morning, as he opened his tent, he noticed his small stool was now laying over as if someone had hit it. He knew it was standing up when he went to bed, but what could have knocked it over without leaving some sign in the leaves or the bare earth around his tent?

If it had been the wind, he would have awoken as it rattled his tent, but he slept through the night. Tom dug what in the military was called a cat hole and relieved his bowels before eating his morning ration. He added his empty ration packages to the hole before covering it up then set about breaking down camp.

By midday Tom had gone farther than the survey crawler had gone before it had to turn back to allow its solar cells to recharge its batteries. At midafternoon he came upon a small stream about a meter wide and roughly a foot deep at this location. He called it in, so it could be located on a map giving compass bearings upstream and downstream for future reference. There were small minnow size fish in the stream, but nothing large enough to eat at this location. The speed of the water flow was gentle, and he tossed a dry leaf in it to get an estimate of its flow.

He walked down the stream for over a kilometer before he found the first fruit since landing. It was berries that look like blackberries he used to pick as a kid in Missouri. He checked them carefully before picking the first one then tested it to insure it was safe to eat. Tom took photos of the bush with the small digital camera he was carrying to document anything he might discover.

Tom advised the settlement of his find and the test results on the berry before eating one. He found it to be sweet with a strong flavor unlike any berry he had ever eaten before. Tom only ate one and considered gathering up some to take back to the settlement, but he decided to leave them, and he could return with a hydrogen powered crawler later to pick them.

He moved back upstream and moved on past his first location to explore the stream some more looking for animal tracks since this was a prime source of water for any animal. He had gone nearly two kilometers before he decided to make camp and had passed several of those berry patches on both sides of the stream.

After he had tested the water, he ran it though his purifier, checked it again then refilled his water supply from it. Tonight,

Tom cleared an area of leaves then built a small fire to heat water, so he could have a hot meal, instead of his normal cold ration. As before he could sense something out of his visual range, but he could never nail it down even using binoculars or night vision goggles.

The next morning his stool was once again knocked over and the ashes of the fire had been disturbed, but still there were no tracks to indicate passage of any type of creature. Tom followed the stream for three days until he found the source. It was a spring bubbling up out of the ground. He camped by the spring and had it pin pointed by the satellites if needed as a water source later. And as with every morning, his campsite was disturbed.

Tom had taken to leaning sticks together and other things just to see if they would be disturbed in the morning. He even staked his empty ration pack to the ground and the next morning the stake was lying beside the hole it left in the ground, and Tom could never find the empty package.

He turned back to his basic compass bearing and moved deeper into the forest. The settlement moved a remote to the edge of the forest suspended in the air six hundred feet above the ground, so they could maintain radio contact.

Nine days into his journey, Tom had discovered three streams and four other berry plants with different formed berries with different flavors. All were very sweet to the tongue and flavorful.

Contact with the settlement gave him his location via satellite tracking and his azimuth back. He considered shooting an azimuth, forty-five degrees off his return path, then correcting his direction to return to where the relay was anchored on the fifteenth day, knowing he had saved a small portion of his rations since he seemed to eat lightly during his midday meal.

As the sun was going down as Tom was sitting, just looking around a glimmer seemed to sparkle in a sun beam in the distance from his location. Tom pulled his binoculars out of his vest and looked at the glimmer. Something about the glimmer said it had form. A form unnatural for its surroundings. He judged it to be about four hundred meters from his position and before the sun moved to remove the glimmer, Tom shot an azimuth with his compass, so he could check it out in the morning.

The next morning Tom kept his routine in eating and clearing his campsite before shooting the azimuth to the glimmer he had seen the previous evening. He took his time constantly searching around him for any danger. For a moment in time he felt as he did on his first patrol in Vietnam walking point. But this time he had no foe which he could recognize.

When Tom was about fifty meters from where he felt the glimmer came from, the form took solid shape. He was looking at the ruins of a building weathered away over unknown years. Tom slowly moved to the remains and saw the source of the glimmer. It looked like a broken piece of a mirror, but when he moved to it, he found it was polished metal.

Tom had moved inside of the ruins as he moved to check out the mirror and found he was standing on layers of leaves and forest debris. The metal that reflected the light was embedded in a partial wall standing roughly a meter high. He took several photos, then moved around the insides of the ruins scuffing his feet to see if he could locate something on the ground that he might take back with him.

He knew what he was doing was poor scientific procedure, but he did not have the tools on hand to properly search the site, but felt he could not leave without something to show to the rest of the crew. Something was almost driving his curiosity to find some artifact within the ruins.

When he felt something hard against the toe of his boot, Tom got down on his knees and used his Marine K-Bar to dig in out the item he stubbed his toe on. It took him a long time before he knew what he had discovered. It was a sword about three feet long with a blade width of about two inches, and maybe a quarter inch thick down the center of the blade. It reminded him of swords English knights carried into battle.

But he could not get a complete look at the sword as it was encrusted in dirt, so he moved out of the ruins and decided to take it back to the last stream he had crossed to wash the dirt from the sword.

When was about twenty meters from the ruins his radio was screaming at him, demanding him to respond to their call.

"Base this is Tom. What's the problem? Over."

"Tom, where have you been? We lost track of you over two hours ago. Over."

"Base I was checking out something I found. You say I've been off the track for two hours. Over."

"Affirmative Tom. Are you alright? You have a pregnant female here about ready to call out the Coast Guard to come and rescue you. Over."

"Advise my bride I am in good health and if you can see me now on the track, give me the azimuth to the last stream I was at. Over."

A few moments went by before they responded.

"Tom. Take an azimuth of 210 degrees. The spring is approximately two thousand meters on that azimuth."

"I copy 210 degrees for two klicks. Over."

"Roger that. Tom, what are your plans now? Over."

"Base, in the morning give me an azimuth from my position to the nearest edge of the tree line. Be advised I must have hit a spot where electronics will not work. I've seen this before on Earth and have to admit, it can be a mess without a good map. Glad the tracking system is working as designed. Out."

Tom tried to shoot the azimuth while holding the sword, but the compass needle kept swinging back and forth until he dropped the sword and moved away from it. Once he had the direction fixed in his head he picked up the sword and moved in the direction of the stream.

He almost missed the spring but remembered how the terrain looked around it. He dropped his pack and lay the sword into the water to let the dirt soak up the water and watched as the flow moved the dirt slowly off the sword downstream. Tom sat and watched as the dirt became mud then watch it floating away.

Soon the definition of the sword came from underneath unknown years of dirt to present a finely crafted sword with jewels in the hilt and pommel. Tom gathered up leaves and began to wipe the sword to remove the remains of the dirt being careful of the edge of the blade which looked as if it had been sharpened that very morning.

Tom took the sword in hand and swung it several times to get a sense of its balance and it felt as if it had been made for his own use. He walked over to a small sapling about two inched thick and swung on it. The blade sliced through it as if it was paper. Tom drove the blade about eight inches into the ground then set up camp for the night. He sat looking at the blade until dark then left is as it was when he went to bed. The next morning, nothing in the camp had been disturbed including his stool which had been knocked over every morning since he had entered the forest.

It would take Tom three days to reach the tree line where he was met by Chief Sharpe on a crawler, twenty-kilometers from the settlement.

The Change

Tom and Chief Sharpe hardly talked on the way back to the settlement during the two-hour trip home. Tom had noticed that the Chief had gave him an odd look as they met, but never said anything other than Asami had been worried about him. He thought the look came from the odd shape he had attached to his pack since he had taken the piece of parachute he had carried to erect additional shelter if needed and had wrapped the sword in it.

The Chief pulled up to the gathering place with everyone waiting for them. Tom saw Asami and when the crawler stopped she took a couple steps towards him then stopped, and just looked at him. He looked at the crowd and they were just staring at him as if he had grown two heads. Tom got off the crawler and walked towards Asami and she stepped back from him.

"Asami, what's wrong?"

"Thomas, take your hat off please."

He had his pack in one hand and his AK-47 in his other hand slung it behind his back then reached up and pulled his bush hat off.

"What's wrong Asami?"

She turned to the crowd.

"Someone get a mirror." She ordered.

Tom just stood looking at Asami as no one moved or spoke as Karen Costello ran to her quarters and returned with an eight-inch makeup mirror and handed it to Asami. Asami walked to her husband and held the mirror up to his face. What Tom saw shocked him. Tom's hair was longer than he would have worn it in the Marine Corps, but it was still short compared to most men and he had not shaved during the trip in the forest. Now instead of the dark brown hair with the beginning of a hint of grey at the temples, his hair was snow white as was his whiskers and mustache.

He stepped around Asami and walked to the tables under the canopy and tossed his pack on one, unhooked his AK from the sling it hung on, and began to unfasten the sword from his pack. Tom lay the sword on the table, then began to unwrap it as the crew began to gather around him.

Tom uncovered the sword and stood in on the table by the point.

"People, we are not the first here, and I don't think we are alone either."

Asami moved to the table and reached out to the sword. Tom grabbed her by the wrist, stopping her from touching it.

"No dear, not with your bare hand. This may be why my hair has turned and God only knows what else has happened to me."

"Thomas, then we need to give you a complete physical and do it now."

"Yes Asami, I understand. Captain Youngerford, I'm going to leave the sword here, but like I said, no one touch it with a bare hand. Something about it just does not feel right. It's almost as if it was made for me since it balances so well in my hand. And the blade is extremely sharp. After my physical, I'll tell the crew where and how I found it."

"Understand Tom. Chief Sharpe, take charge of the sword and examine it carefully. Michael, since you are our Geologist see if you can determine the classification of gemstones." Captain Youngerford was talking to Michael Lathrop the mission Geologist.

"Let's go Asami. If I'm alright, then we have some kissing to make up for. If not, then we need to work out the logistics of the problem." Tom spoke to his wife.

Asami, Doctor Ostrow and Karen Costello escorted Tom to the Medical Module for a complete physical while Chief Sharpe carefully took the sword to the Maintenance Module to run tests on the sword's metal. Michael Lathrop would wait his turn with the gemstones once the Chief had made his tests.

It took two hours to complete a full physical on Tom with Karen running his blood through every test they had available. Every test ran on Tom came back within norms for a man his age and physical condition, and the results were close to being identical to his test results when he first arrived at Houston. They could not find a single thing which would explain why his hair had turned white. An MRI showed no deformities in his brain or elsewhere in his body.

Everyone met under the canopy once Tom's physical was complete and the Chief and Lathrop had made their initial estimates of the sword. First Tom told how he found the sword and the effects he felt while in the ruins. He said in looking back he felt a bit of apprehension as he entered the ruins, but once inside it was as if he knew something was there to be found.

Chief Sharpe said he had no idea what kind of metal the blade was made off as it nearly destroyed a file made from a super-alloy which could shave metal from the hardest metals on Earth. Michael Lathrop said he had never seen stones of the type found in the handle or pommel of the sword, and without removing them, he could not make a positive identification of them.

Tom gave his small camera to Paul McCabe, so he could download the photos he had taken, then gave the small bottles he had collected the different berries in to Raelyn Silvers, their Horticulturists who would be assisted by Nadia Konoval to run tests on to determine value for the settlement. He did say he had tasted one of each of the berries after he had run the tests to insure they were safe to eat.

After a communal evening meal, Tom took his gear to their home, cleaned everything needing attention then made love to Asami. He lay in their bed later thinking about what had happened to him, yet he did not feel any different except he was tired.

The next day Tom assisted the Chiefs as they gathered up trees which had been cut down along the edge of the forest for sawing into lumber for new, larger homes for the settlement. The saw mill had been set up during the first week Tom was in the forest and the cutting of the trees during the rest of his time exploring the forest.

Tom took the afternoon to finally assemble his own crawler utilizing one of the hydrogen motors from a module. Asami assisted him as she told stories about what had happened while he was gone and that she was being careful in doing things now that she was expecting. Tom knew that she was observing him to see if something else cropped up that was not detected. He finally asked her if that was what she was doing, and she admitted that was one reason, but the other reason was she really missed him.

Evening dinner was baked fish from the inland sea which produced a white, flaky meat similar to Earth's White Bass. Discussion under the canopy found itself centered on Tom's search of the forest and he described the incidents with his stool and other tale-tells he had set up to detect the passage of any creature through his camps.

Tom finally voiced his concern that with the large, grassy plain they were settled on and a large body of fresh water nearby, there was zero sign of animal life moving to graze, feed upon grazers or movement to the water. Then the fact there were no birds to eat the insects or berries. Something just did not feel right.

The Ruins

Asami knew that the change Tom had gone through was affecting him in ways she only saw at night. He had dreams which he was speaking to some unknown person and his words were never intelligible as he seemed to whisper or mumble them in his sleep. He ate as well as the others and he worked hard regardless of the task and never seemed to be weakened by it but once he laid down to sleep it took him almost immediately.

The sword Tom had brought back hung on the wall of their small home fixed in a way, so it would not fall and cause a problem for Asami. She would often look at it trying to determine what it held that caused the change in Tom. As her pregnancy progress he became more and more attentive of her wellbeing often chiding her for doing things normal for a woman in her condition.

Every morning he told her he loved her before they separated for the days tasks and every evening in bed before sleep took them he would tell her again he loved her. She could almost feel his desires to make sure she knew how he felt and it was beginning to worry her.

The daily work schedule was structured around a seven-day work week as it was on Earth, and Sunday was a day of rest for the crew. The crew was slowly pairing off, but there were still four men and five women yet to declare partnership. For Tom, he often took one of the Zodiac boats out onto the inland sea on Sunday, and fished for hours by himself always staying in sight of land as per Asami's request. Asami knew he was using that time to think about what had happened to him and what the future held for them.

Asami was five months pregnant when she awoke one night to find Tom standing in front of the sword staring at it. The sword seemed to glow in the darkness and when he turned back to their bed it seemed to dull. This frightened her more than anything they had already experienced. At first, she thought Tom was asleep as he was standing there, until he spoke to her as he was getting back in bed.

"Asami, I need to go back to the ruins. Something is missing from this place and the ruins might hold the secret. That sword is part of a message, yet it is incomplete."

"Thomas, I'm scare for you."

"I know you are baby, I'm scared too honey. But I think for the sake of our child, and the other children to be born here, I must do this."

"Then I'll go with you."

"No Asami. I'll not risk you and our child because of what is becoming an obsession. But somewhere inside of me is the feeling I will return to you. Honey, I have not been this scared since the first time I walked point in Vietnam."

"Thomas, I know this is not a macho thing for you, but can you give me a simple explanation of what is happening from your view point. I mean that sword glowing as it was as you looked at it is something completely foreign."

"All I can tell you is that it seemed to be talking to me, telling me to return to the Ruins as if I left an important piece there which is vital to our survival. If it was just me I could ignore what I can only call a summons. But I took on the job of protecting the crew, and if this is what it takes to accomplish that mission, then I have no other choice but to do it."

She took his hand and laid it upon her swollen belly.

"If we have a son, what do you wish to name him?"

"Honey, if it is alright with you I'd like to name him Carl Wayne after my father."

"Carl Wayne Jenkins. Yes, that is a good name for a male child. And if it is a girl?"

"I give you that privilege."

"I'd like to name her Yoshie after my mother who was the driving force behind me going to medical school. If I had not gone to medical school, we would have never met. Yoshie Marie Jenkins is a good name I think."

"It's a wonderful name Asami. Now go to sleep, the day will soon be upon us and there are things to do."

Tom laid out his plans to return to the Ruins to the crew at the communal morning meal. Several of the men and women made it known they would go with him, but he shut them down saying this was a risk only he could take. Once he convinced the crew this was the best course of action, they got down to planning for his trip.

His crawler was equipped with a pressure tank for enough hydrogen gas to take him to and from the Ruins. He would drag a small trailer containing a small hydrogen fracker in case he needed additional fuel, plus a tethered balloon to raise on site, so he would have radio communications with the settlement.

Tools for excavating the Ruins plus a video camera attached to the crawler which could be remotely activated so the crew could observe his actions from a distance. Tom made a scabbard for the sword from wood bound together with parachute cord and a waist band made from nylon strapping from a pod.

The night before he left they made slow, gentle love being considerate of Asami's condition.

They ate breakfast in their cramped quarters before he left an hour before sunrise. Tom wanted to get to the Ruins as early as possible and he knew the terrain could be rough in spots, plus he wanted to bypass the streams where possible in order not to damage the flow by creating a pool with the indents of his crawler tracks.

He entered the forest before sunrise and was grateful of the halogen lights on the crawler lighting his way. As he passed different berry bushes, he took a moment to check how full the branches were, so he could pick them on his return home. He had several plastic tubs with lids in the trailer for that very purpose. The tests on the samples he had returned with proved safe for human consummation, and Tom was asked to bring a sprig or two back for transplanting if possible.

Tom only stopped once during this trip to eat at midday. Unlike his first trip, he was not concerned with what might be around him, hiding beneath the leaf covered forest floor or behind a bush. The sword was in the front of the crawler with him as was his AK-47 clipped into its transport rack.

He checked his watch when he arrived to see the time it took for him to arrive. I was three forty-seven which was almost a lie since the rotation of the planet was off enough to make it add time to a day that did not exist. He checked the computer link in the crawler to see it was two thirty-one based upon the adjustment in time to account for the rotation. He reset his watch then just looked at the Ruins it had taken him nine days on foot to find.

Fear eased from his soul as he looked at a place that had been haunting him since his return to the settlement. Tom took the sword from its resting place, pulled it from the scabbard and walked to the ruins. He knew the video camera was recording what he was doing but he had not yet raised the relay, so the settlement would see his actions.

Tom walked to where he had found the sword and drove it into the ground then listened for anything to warn him his actions were being watched. The feeling of being watched had been strong from the first moment he had set foot in the forest and it persisted today.

He went back to the crawler and filled the balloon with hydrogen, then carefully let it rise through the trees to approximately six hundred feet, then checked the radio link back to the settlement. Once he knew he was tied to the settlement via the radio and camera, he took a rake from the trailer and went into the Ruins and began to rake the leaf debris from the inside of the Ruins, so he could begin to excavate them. After he had all the leafy debris checked for artifacts and removed, he used parachute cord and began to lay out a grid pattern inside the Ruins, so he could document exactly were any item discovered was located within the Ruins. This was sound scientific principal which he had not been able to use the first time within the Ruins.

He was using gardening tools to clear one grid after another scrapping the earth to loosen it and remove it using a collapsible bucket to carry the soil outside the Ruins. Depending on what he found on this trip, it was considered that making a shifter and pumping water to the Ruins to wash the removed soil to find anything that might be hidden within the soil from human eyes.

Tom cleared three inches of soil from the first grid without finding anything then moved to the next. From time to time he would look at the piece of jagged metal jutting from partial wall of the Ruins that had glimmered in the light to tell him of the Ruins and considered by passing what he was doing and chisel that piece of metal from the wall, but something kept telling him the real secrets were buried beneath his feet.

It was not until the third grid that he began to find bits and pieces of metal. He photographed each piece as best he could and put them in a small plastic tub he had brought. In the trailer was another larger tub and five gallons of water just for cleaning anything he found in the dirt. Once he had cleared the grid he took the items he found to the trailer and cleaned them, then took a photo of them.

It was getting late by the time he had finished cleaning the artifacts, so he made camp. He spoke with the settlement and Asami before shutting down the crawler's systems to conserve its batteries, then turned in for the night.

Tom slept peacefully through the night and awoke somewhat refreshed. He ate his morning meal as he waited for the sun to rise enough to provide him with light within the Ruins. He ran the crawler's motor long enough for the gauges to show a full charge on the batteries then went to work.

Grid by grid he cleared the floor of the Ruins until he came to the grid next to the sword. The bits and pieces of metal and what looked like pottery he was finding became larger, and some with more definition than others, but nothing yet to give him a solid look at what this Ruins were about. It took time digging then cleaning and photographing the artifacts, but it was a proper scientific method. With every grid photographed he sent the photos back via his comm link and moved to the next. He was as close to being Archaeologist in the crew with his degree in Geography.

He was at his dig depth on the grid next to the sword when he hooked something with the prongs of the small hand cultivator he was using to break up the soil. It looked like a chain of some sort and he carefully dug around it with his hands until he could lift it from the soil without straining the links. He photographed it then went directly to the wash tub and cleaned it using a toothbrush and small paint brush.

Even though the metal was stained from years in the ground it appeared to be a gold chain with a medallion almost three inches in diameter. He went to his pack and took out the toothpaste from it and went back to use it on the medallion. Soon the medallion gleamed from the polishing action of the toothpaste. Centered in it was engraved a dragon with markings around the perimeter of the medallion unknown to him. He cleaned the back the same way to find similar writings on it. He left the chain as it was and just looked at the medallion. It almost felt warm in his hands as he held it.

Tom walked to the sword and compared the engravings with those on the sword's blade and recognized they were the same. He would never be able to explain what he did next, but he hung the medallion on the sword, then sat down and looked at it.

There was a feeling of peace slowly filling his body as he just looked at the medallion hanging from the sword as if it belonged there. What happened next was completely unexpected.

The Path

Emily Turner, the crews Ophthalmologist was on duty in the Command Module watching the monitor as Tom moved to the sword and placed the medallion on it. She zoomed the cameras lens onto the medallion, then gave a broadcast call to the crew the Tom had found something. Soon the module filled with crew members wanting to see what Tom had found.

Once everyone had a good look via the monitor, all but Asami and Captain Youngerford returned to their chores to complete the days' tasks. The crops were growing well and the harvest of some of the vegetables needed to be attended too. Others would be left to go to seed so they could repeat the planting using those seeds instead of the store of seeds they still had put away.

Tom just continued to sit, looking at the medallion trying to determine a reason for such things on a planet which seemed to be void of life above the insect level. He felt the light breeze which flowed through the forest seem to lightly increase, changing direction and into his face. Something was moving out of his visual range, but he could feel, almost hear what sounded like footsteps in the rustling of the leave on the forest floor.

He seemed to come out of nowhere as Tom watched an aged man moved through the forest to the Ruins. Tom stood as he watched the old man moved gracefully in his purple robe and what appeared to be a gold, ankle length gown beneath the robe. The old man stepped into the Ruins seeming to ignore the grid lines which would trip a normal man. When he spoke to Tom it felt like a combination of tingling metal and ice flowing through Tom's veins.

"Master Gunnery Sergeant Thomas Allan Jenkins. We have been waiting for you."

"Who are you Sir?"

"My name is not one readily translated to your language, but for the sake of this meeting, please call me Arthur."

"Thank you, Arthur. I returned here as soon as I could find the courage to do so. I apologize if I kept you waiting too long."

"Thomas, you misunderstand. We have been waiting thousands of your years for you. Or a man like you. Welcome to the world we call Haven."

"Why have you been waiting for one like me, and what makes me so special?"

"Thomas, you are unique amongst those of earth. You are intelligent, yet you have only used that intelligence for the gain of others instead of yourself. You gave up a great love so that individual would not suffer because of that love. There is so much more about you that I could describe, but time will not allow it."

"I may have given up a great love on Earth, but I found an even greater one in Asami. But how do you know so much about me?"

"Simple, we have watched you as your vessel flew through space. We entered your unconscious mind to see the memories stored there to learn what manner of people were brave enough to leave the safety of their world to explore a new world."

"Who are you that you can do that?"

"In a very ancient Earth tongue, we were once called the Yahweh. We are creatures who once walked your planet to guide the evolution of your species, but things became confused, and some of our people showed a tendency for violent action, creating many disasters which we as a species would have preferred never happened. We left your species with myths and legends to fend for themselves knowing we had ruined what was an honest experiment."

"Arthur, I am confused."

"That is understandable, but it will all become clear in time. But we shall not interfere more than we already have with the life you have begun here. I will say this. There will be two events that will soon take place that will require your strength to insure the survival of your settlement. Another group of humans left your Earth fifty years after you left, and we have assisted in advancing their travel across space to arrive before your second year here is done."

"You have such power?"

"Yes, it was a minor thing to accomplish. Thomas, we intercepted your vessel and guided it here for a purpose. We fixed the things on your vessel that nature itself tried to destroy. All of you would have died in space if we had not interfered and would have starved once you arrived if we had not preserved your food stores."

"If you prevented us from dying in space, then why did we lose a crew member? Roger Lindstrom?"

"We allowed Roger Lindstrom to die because in looking into his mind, he wanted your lover Asami. He was willing to kill you to have her. Even before you left Earth he was plotting for you to be involved in an accident to end your life. We calculated he had a forty percent chance of success which was unacceptable to us, so we insured he would not survive to carry out his plans."

Tom stood and thought about Lindstrom and how friendly he always seemed, but if what this man had told him was true, then all he could do was accept it at face value and move on. But it would be a secret he would not divulge to the crew.

"Arthur, you said two incidents. What is the second?"

"Your Earth is not what it once was. It is one you would not recognize nor wish to live on. But those of Earth have discovered how to cover vast distances of space in a short time. They have detected the signal from your vessel and have determined the location of your settlement's planet. We miscalculated in this or we would never have allowed that to happen. They are coming, and you will have to deal with them."

"If you can arrange for my vessel and the following one to find Haven, then can you not prevent them from finding us?"

"That was considered before our Council, but it does not follow the path we have set you on. No Thomas, it will be you, and you alone that will prevent this other group from destroying what you are so intent on building."

"How can I fight a people who will have weapons far superior to my own?"

"You have everything you need before you Thomas Jenkins. The red stone in the pommel of that sword is called a Dragon's Eye, and will give you everything you need to defeat an enemy if you are brave enough to use it. It is more powerful than any weapon you can imagine, and it will give itself to you without cost to you or those you care for. But to not use it will cost all that you love. Together with the medallion, you can prevent the destruction of all you value."

"How does it work?"

"That is for you to learn. But time is short. Do not be timid."

"Arthur, I still do not understand?"

"Thomas, we created you and the situation you are now in and will find yourself in later, but we have decided for you to walk the path before you with only the help of the tools given to you. We have heard your voices asking why there is no life on Haven other than the insects and that is being corrected as we speak. We were not sure exactly how your people would handle landing on a planet without a ready supply of food, so we removed all animal life from the planet except for the fish in the sea. You will recognize the life we will return to you as life found on your planet, except that we have excluded the dangerous animals which you knew from Earth. Those were placed there by those of my people who had evil intent. We shall not make that mistake twice."

"No dangerous animals? So, there are no predators to help control the other animal populations?"

"No Thomas we control that. As you harvest we will replenish from deeper in the forest so there will always be game available, yet not such a large animal population which will stress the environment."

Tom looked at the sword and medallion before looking back at Arthur.

"Thomas to answer your unasked question, my race is immortal. I have walked across the face of your planet many times before even the dawn of humanity. The last thing I shall say about why you chosen is that in your memories you have killed many men in battle, and deep inside you hated yourself for that action, yet you only did so to protect those you were with. If you must kill to protect your wife and children, then we accept that as a last resort on your part. We will not meet again Thomas until the day of your last breath. Peace be with you Thomas Jenkins."

With that Arthur faded away leaving Thomas with the feeling he had been talking to a ghost. He looked around at the Ruins to see them crumbling before his eyes, yet the sword and medallion stood before him as he had set them.

He removed the medallion from the sword and placed it into the leg pouch of his field pants, then pulled the sword from the ground and carefully wiped the dirt from the blade. Tom raised the sword up and looked at the stone set in the pommel and it seemed to twinkle in the late afternoon light and he felt it was his own imagination that it had spoken to him.

"Yes Master, I await your command."

As he walked back to the crawler he heard his radio crackle asking for him to respond. When he responded he was told they had watched him stand up then the video and radio feed became distorted until it returned as he removed the medallion from the sword. Tom told them everything was fine, and he would return the next day.

The next morning Tom was awakened to the sound of birds singing in the trees. He stopped at three different berry patches and filled the tubs he had brought along for that purpose. During those stops he began to see animals moving through the forest. Squirrels barking in the trees, rabbits moving about looking for a green leaf to eat on and an elk moving to water further down the steam he was at.

He returned late in the day with his bounty of berries. They were washed and several large bowls of them were laid out to go with the evening communal meal where Tom told what he felt was necessary to the crew. Tom told of how they had been helped in their journey to what would now be called Haven, but he left out the death of Roger Lindstrom or the fact danger was approaching from deep space.

Tom told them they were on their own as far as the aliens who had helped them to this point. He left many questions posed to him unanswered as he said he just did not know. He hated to lie to the people who were now his family, but felt in time it would make their lives easier than knowing the truth.

The sword went back on the wall and the medallion was completely cleaned and buffed while it was being studied, then it was hung on the wall next to the sword.

Asami noticed that never again did Tom have strange dreams or nightmares, and the stone in the sword never glowed as it had the night Tom decided to return to the Ruins.

The Arrival

The days seemed to be endless with the work needing to be accomplished for the settlement to survive and grow. Everyone wondered if this was what it was like for the early settlers of North America coming from Europe to carve out a place to live in the wilderness.

When they had enough dried lumber, a meeting house was built on the pad in place of the parachute canopy. It was complete with one of the small kitchens that was extra along with toilet facilities. This was for the communal meals, even as the crew was pairing off.

Also, the communications and computers from the command module were placed into the communal hall and the command module was moved away to be disassembled when time permitted.

Lauren Randall, their Chemical Engineer decided that she would remain single and allow the others to pair up and mate. She only made one request and that was when she determined she was ready, then Tom provide her with his sperm via artificial insemination, so she could provide a child to the growth of the settlement. Tom accepted her offer especially since the child would carry the Jenkins name at birth.

The first year came and went without any celebration except for everyone, except Asami, enjoying a glass of wine made from the berries that were being harvested in the forest. The Chiefs had built the apparatus for turning the berries into wine, and even harder spirits under the supervision of Lauren to insure quality and taste.

Asami gave birth to a strong son while the communal building was being erected and Captain Youngerford suggested that the first house to be built would be the home of Tom and Asami, since they now needed more room because of the baby.

The growing of the animal embryos was disappointing in that they were barely achieving a twenty percent success rate. Because they now had to let what stock was surviving, bred and grow larger herds before they would have fresh meat, Tom went hunting. He took a large bull elk in the forest, then a month later he went further east on the continent where he took a bison cow. One of the modules had been outfitted with everything needed to butcher cattle along with a walk-in freezer to preserve the meats from harvesting the stock they were projected to grow.

Baby Carl was four months old when three of the women announced they were pregnant. When Tom was not busy, he could be found playing with Carl as he was just beginning to learn to crawl. If he could safely deal with him, Tom would take Carl on his trips to collect berries or hunt with Carl strapped into a baby seat that Chief Green had designed and made from wood.

Carl was almost six months old when he woke his parents late one night from his crib at the foot of their bed. Their new house was not ready to move into yet and Carl was making a lot of racket as he had climbed up the side of his crib and was shaking it. What was causing his racket was the Dragon Stone in the sword was glowing.

Tom and Asami got out of bed with Asami going to Carl and picking him up, as Tom went to the sword. He looked at it for a moment, then reached over and gripped the medallion. With his other hand he touched the hilt of the sword and could feel a surge of energy flowing through his body, then a voice in his head.

"Master, there is a vessel in orbit containing your people. Do you wish them to join you as you came to Haven, or be placed safely away from here without harm?"

Tom never spoke openly, just closed his eyes and pictured an area about a kilometer away to the east where he wished the new comers to land.

"It shall be done Master."

The glow subsided, and Tom released the medallion, then the sword before turning to Asami.

"Asami, I have to go. We have company coming and we must prepare for them."

"Company? Who Thomas?"

"Another expedition from Earth."

"How do you know about that?"

"Arthur told me about them, but not when they would arrive. I kept that information from you and the others because I was not sure when they would arrive."

"And the glowing stone told you they had arrived?"

"Yes. There is a lot I have not spoken of, but I have to go attend to this in person. Asami trust me in that I have no choice in this, but to be deal with this in person."

"Alright Thomas, but please find the time to explain it all to me someday. This frightens me not knowing what you are involved in."

Tom moved to Asami, kissed her, then kissed Carl on the forehead. Carl reached up and grabbed a handful of the beard Tom had grown and pulled on it as if demanding another kiss which Tom planted on his cheek. Tom got dressed and put the medallion around his neck under his t-shirt, so it would be touching his skin.

He took the sword down from the wall and slipped it into its scabbard, then put the strap over his shoulder. His hair was now shoulder length and still snow white, but instead of putting on his bush hat as he always did, he just brushed it back with his hands, looked at Asami, winked at her and left their small home.

Asami stepped out of their home to see Tom turn away from the communal hall where the night watch was located and walked towards the east. She went back into the house, got dressed then wrapped Carl in a light blanket, then went to the communal hall to advise the night watch that Tom had left to deal with a new group of Earthlings that were arriving.

Peter Moran was on the watch and buzzed Captain Youngerford's quarters. Youngerford came to the hall as soon as he could get dressed and Asami briefed him on what Tom had told her. Youngerford had all the crew awaken, then just waited until they arrived so Asami could also brief them. She never spoke of the glowing stone in the sword, only that Tom seemed to know about the new arrivals and that he had left on foot to the east.

It was three hours before sunrise and a morning meal was made up while everyone just waited for sunrise and talked amongst themselves.

Tom stood in the pre-dawn darkness and watched as one, then another, then another module, floated to earth without parachutes and were neatly lined up in two rows. He counted fifty modules in all resting peacefully in front of him. These modules were half again as large as the ones that had brought the Morbius Expedition to Haven and in his mind, he could see they were tightly packed with humans in thirty of them.

Thirty modules containing twenty-five pods each meant there were seven hundred and seventy-five new people to deal with and feed. Plus, they were still in hibernation at the moment of landing.

Tom gripped the hilt of the sword and closed his eyes and focused on the stone.

"Yes Master?"

"Wake them up gently. They have a big surprise ahead of them once awake."

117

"Yes Master, it shall be as you require."

"And stay linked to me until I order you otherwise."

"Yes Master."

A few minutes passed before the stone spoke again.

"Master sadly it seems thirteen did not survive the journey."

"Thank you. Do you have a name?"

"Master, I have been called many names over the eons, but I will accept any name you wish to call me."

Within Tom's mind flashed a series of scenes where the sword was being yielded in battle. Tom smiled knowing the one name everyone knew, but decided that was for another time.

"I shall call you Simon."

"Yes Master, Simon as in the child's game."

"Yes Simon, that is as good as any reason. Now assist these new people within reason without letting them know of your existence."

"Yes Master."

Tom just stood watching as flashes from insides the modules came to him from time to time as the new arrivals were getting themselves organized. Much like the Morbius crew, they were somewhat disoriented at first, then confused by already being on the ground instead of in space as per the flight program. Tom pulled his radio from his vest and tuned it to the frequency the command crew was using to talk to the individual modules and listened to the cross talk as they tried to get some order to their situation.

As he was listening to the chatter on the radio, Asami walked up beside him with Carl in a chest carrier and stood quietly waiting for Tom to notice them.

"Asami, what are you doing here? It's not safe."

"Thomas, your son would not let me put him in his crib. He spoke his first words and he was all but screaming 'da' and would not be quiet until I started this way. We also brought you a sandwich since you did not eat anything before leaving the house."

Tom looked at Carl who was looking up at him and rustled his hair causing Carl to laugh.

"Alright honey, but if things turn nasty, run like hell. And thanks for the sandwich."

Neither spoke as Tom took his time eating the elk steak sandwich she had brought him. He pulled a piece of stick candy made from a red berry and gave it to Carl, who immediately began to chew on it as he was teething.

Soon a camera came up from the command module and scanned the surrounding area then stopped and focused on Tom and Asami. Tom keyed his radio.

"This is Master Gunnery Sergeant Jenkins, Security Officer of the Morbius Expedition. Who are you? Over."

There was a long pause before he was answered.

"This is the Prometheus Expedition. Colonel John Simmons commanding. Did you say the Morbius Expedition? Over."

"Affirmative. When you get yourselves together, come on out, the weather is fine today. Over."

This caused Asami to giggle since the weather was always fine during the day. Any rain they received only came at night and was clear by daylight. Tom figured this was weather control by the aliens who developed this planet.

119

Thirty minutes later the main hatch on the command module opened and a blond-haired man in a green jumpsuit stepped from the hatch and then onto the ground. Behind him came another man with a flag on a staff. They both walked towards Tom and stopped about four meters in front of him. The man with the flag removed the covering from it and drove the flag pole into the ground. The flag was not an American flag nor was it one Tom had ever seen.

"Master Gunnery Sergeant Jenkins. We have come to claim this planet for the United Earth Federation."

Tom smiled and pointed to the flag. It burst into flames as did the pole.

"Colonel, the name of this planet is Haven. We are not the first to occupy it, nor shall it be claimed for any faction on Earth. The year on Earth is 8338, so your United Earth Federation no longer exists. Now if I was you, I'd reconsider your approach to how you deal with those of us already here."

The Colonel looked at the smoldering remains of his flag and pole then looked back at Tom.

"There were only twenty-four members of the Morbius Expedition. There are over seven hundred of us."

"Actually, there are seven hundred and sixty-two of you. Consider if you will that you are on Haven without the use of a single parachute and your modules are neatly lined up. Do you need any other incentive to cooperate with the residents of Haven?"

"Master, a weapon is rising from the top of the module."

"I see it Simon. If it fires, make sure we are safe and the individual who fires the weapon pays for his stupidity." Tom responded without speaking.

"Yes Master."

"Simon, stop calling me master. Tom is agreeable with me."

"Yes Tom, as you wish."

"Now Colonel, if that weapon which just rose from your module fires, you'll learn just how serious I take your threat of being outnumbered."

"You're standing there with a pistol on your vest and a sword at your side and you think you can convince me that you are able to stop us from claiming this world?"

The Colonel reached up to touch his ear bud, then looked at Tom. He listened again to whatever was coming over his frequency then took a deep sigh.

"I don't know how you are doing it, but none of my people can exit their modules, and life support has been shut down on each of them."

"Colonel Simmons, I do not wish to harm anyone, but you have set the tone of this meeting not I. You came from your module placing yourself in command of an established settlement originating from the same planet, and have tried to bully me into allowing you to take command of our world. You and your people are free to settle here alongside us, but under our rules not yours. Our world on Earth no longer exists, and because of that, we are in danger from yet another expedition which will threaten all our security. You have approximately thirty minutes before the air runs out in the modules and all your people die. But once you make your decision it is yours to live with, or die with, because any attempt later to bring harm to the settlement will be dealt with in a manner too violent to even consider."

"Who are you?"

"I was a United States Marine. This is my wife, Doctor Asami Jenkins and our son Carl. Carl is the first child of this new world. Time is running out Colonel."

The frequencies the modules were using changed back to the one Tom had been monitoring and he could hear the panic in the voices of the people inside them. Tom turned to look at Carl and touched the side of his face. Asami and Simon were almost in concert as they called a warning out. The man with the Colonel had drawn his sidearm and was pointing it at them.

Tom looked at the individual pointing the pistol at them and smile. The man screamed, then seemed to melt before them then caught fire as his screams became louder until his voice was consumed by the fire. Suddenly the weapon on top of the module exploded, and screams could be heard emitting from inside the command module.

"WHO ARE YOU?" The Colonel screamed.

"I told you Colonel. I am Thomas Jenkins, the Security Officer for the Morbius Expedition. Beyond that you are not cleared for any additional information. Twenty-four minutes Colonel."

"Thomas what just happened? Everything is a blur in front of me and I cannot hear anything." Asami quietly asked.

"Nothing to concern yourself with my love."

"Thank you Simon."

"I felt it was proper Tom."

The Colonel looked at what remained of his aide then slowly removed his pistol and dropped it to the ground.

"Mister Jenkins, I surrender to your terms."

"My terms are simple Colonel. Live in peaceful cooperation and support of your fellow man or woman as it may be. Any act of violence will be harshly dealt with. Respect the planet and do not take from it more than you need. I'll explain more once all your people are out of their modules, so they will all receive the same information at the same time. Their conduct rests on your shoulders Colonel."

Tom turned away from the Colonel and offered his arm to Asami. They walked away as Tom listened to the Colonel tell his people to leave all weapons inside the modules when they exited. He never looked back as Simon spoke to him.

"Have no fears Tom. No weapon can harm you today or forever as long as you are in contact with the medallion."

"Simon, my fears are for my wife and child."

*"Tom, I can only protect them when they are close to you as they are today. I am truly sorry, but it is as it is, I can do no more."

"I understand Simon. Thank you for your honesty."

Later that morning Tom returned to speak with the new arrivals. As he had told his own crew they were on this planet because the people who had constructed it wanted them there. When questioned about the power he held, he only told them the power came from their sponsors and he held a grave responsibility in caring for it. He regretted the deaths of the people that morning, but they were warned to do no harm yet ignored such a warning. Violence against another would not be tolerated and he had no control over the punishment of the offenders.

Tom reminded them of how many years had passed since they had left Earth and that the world they left was no longer a place for people such as themselves. They had to adjust their way of thinking as they made a new home on Haven or perish. The choice was theirs.

He mingled with the new people answering questions the best he could and trying to get a handle on what brought them to this world. Simon was whispering in his ear from time to time that there was a sense of defeat in some and defiance in others. Only time would determine if these people would accept this world as given to them or try to change it into the Earth they had left.

Two days later a group met with Tom and the Morbius crew in the communal hall. Colonel Simmons was present, but it was obvious he was no longer in charge. Tom's first meeting had cost this crew three men who had defied his warnings and the manner of their deaths and the fact they had been locked in their modules with a decreasing oxygen supply had tempered any aggression on conquering this new land.

During the meeting, Simon warned of one of the people attending the meeting intended harm once they were settled, in order to further the purpose of their own expedition. Tom told Simon to deal with the man in due time without real harm to him since it was time to show some compassion in dealing with these new people.

Tom waited until the meeting was near complete when he challenged the man to express his intentions for the future. He was a mining engineer who figured on getting rich on a new world and now his plans were being thwarted by Tom and he did not intend to be turned away from his goal.

As the man lied about his intentions, he began to feel pain in his joints. The more he lied the greater the pain as it spread throughout his body until he collapsed onto the floor from his seat. Tom moved to stand over him as everyone moved away afraid he would burst into flames like the others had the day before.

"Sir, do not think you can deceive us. Your talents can be of great value to this world, but within reason. All you desire is to destroy what exists for your own gain. This world will not permit such a thing. How you spend your life is your choice. In pain or in a spirit of living with the world as given to you."

The man cried out he would change. He would live within the guidelines set down if the pain would go away. Instantly he found relief with Tom looking down at him.

"Remember that pain as it will return if you go back on your word. And the next time it will be permanent."

As Tom moved back to his own chair he could see the fear in the faces of everyone in hall including his own crew. He just sat down and contemplated what he had done. Had he just become the kind of person he always hated? He never spoke another word as the meeting broke up with his crew remaining in the hall. They were silent for a long time before Captain Youngerford spoke.

"Tom, what's happened to you?"

"Captain, I wish I could tell you, but I promise you this. You have nothing to fear from me. But we are greatly outnumbered by the new arrivals and they are not the same as us. Earth changed while we were gone, and these new people do not hold the same values as we do. Forgive me but I am tired."

"Tom, what do you want us to do now?"

"Captain, I'm only your Security Officer. I am sworn to protect the crew. You are still in command as far as I am concerned outside of that so what you do next is up to you."

Tom stood, picked up the sword off the table then offered his hand to Asami who took it then walked out of the hall in silence. At home he laid down on the bed and Carl crawled up to him and curled up with him as Asami just sat and watched them go to sleep. She was scared of what was happening to Tom, and knew that she could only stand back and watch as it played out.

Passage of Time

Progress cannot be stopped except in cases where there was nothing to progress to and on a new world there was much to do and achieve. The new people settled in with the guidance of the Morbius crew in building a community around the Morbius settlement.

The equipment they brought with them was lighter and better able to deal with many of the daily tasks needing to be done. Truck size crawlers were assembled which helped bring timber to the saw mill which had been enlarged with a new, more capable saw to make lumber. There was no need to clear cut the forest to provide for farm land as once was done on Earth, and Chief Sharpe oversaw the harvest of timber insuring the new growth would be able to grow for future use.

The plain was only plowed to provide enough food for the community plus some in reserve and seed for future plantings. Using the metals and parts from the modules a rock crusher was constructed to provide crushed gravel for road and walkways throughout the community.

The new arrivals brought with them newer techniques for raising cattle from the embryos both groups brought and soon a large heard of beef cattle roamed the plains. Horses were raised and the platoon of soldiers that were brought with the new arrivals became the cowboys who cared for the cattle and other food stock.

Lauren Randall who had exempted herself from pairing up with a mate found a man in the new group that was also a Chemical Engineer, and they mated to provide the first child from the mixed community. Soon the community was growing by an average of five children a month.

Tom found he had little to do as the new people took over chores he always attended to, and as he moved amongst the community he was often referred to as Sheriff Jenkins. His hair and bread were long now, and his face was deeply tanned giving him an odd contrast between the white hair and beard and the dark skin.

As Carl grew, he was often found riding on his father's shoulders as he toured the various activities around the settlement. The people Carl interacted with found him to be very articulate and very intelligent for his age. He was curious about everything, but even when standing on his own, he was careful in what he was looking or asking about. Unlike a normal child with a curious nature, Carl did not approach anything he was unsure of, and Tom just let him explore, but never out of his sight.

A new hospital was built with fifty beds due to the increase of settlers and was always at least half full with normal medical problems, and women giving birth. Carl was five when Asami announced she was once again expecting which Carl took as great news since he would have a baby brother to play with. When Asami told Carl, he might have a sister, Carl was adamant that he would have a brother and would not accept it any other way. Tom silently laughed at the way Carl had told his mother to make sure he had a brother.

Engineering committees were formed to take what they had brought with them to improve their daily lives. The hydrogen engines were providing power to everything that moved, but they were also dangerous and three had exploded injuring the operators. No deaths had occurred yet, but it was only time before that happened.

Drilling equipment had been added to the Prometheus Expedition for drilling for water and once assembled, trial holes were drilled searching for fossil fuels. Once oil was discovered, a small refinery was built with care of spillage to produce fuels and lubricants for the machinery needed to grow the settlement.

Tom's function as Security Officer became one of Law Enforcement within the settlement. A City Council was formed by election and developed guidelines and laws for the community.

Tom was always in attendance to the meetings and only expressed his opinion when asked. Tom's early display of his abilities had all but stopped any form of violence, but as he had instructed Simon, all he was concerned with was planned violence. Two people getting into a physical disagreement due to a sudden loss of temper was not to be dealt with in any fashion except by the leadership.

Once Tom learned he did not have to carry the sword to be linked to it, he kept it on the wall of his home. Simon informed him that no one could remove the sword without injury which caused Tom some concern since Asami, or even Carl might touch it. Simon assured Tom that neither of them would be harmed if such an event occurred.

Tom kept his word to Asami in that once there were meats to be processed, he had a portion seasoned and cured according to the recipes to make the Schlotzsky's sandwiches. Carl was hesitant at first to try this odd meal his parents were eating, but fell in love with the mustard that enriched the flavor of the meal. Asami only cried at first when she saw the meal, remembering what Tom had said to her on their first date.

A school was built near the hospital with Carl being its oldest student in pre-school. Asami thought Carl would fight going to school since he seemed to always want to be with Tom during the day, but he was ready to go and learn things the first day, and was pleased that there were other children there to play with.

Tom and Asami were planning a birthday party for Carl's sixth birthday when Tom looked like he was stricken by illness. What Tom was feeling was dread as Simon announced that a group of three Earth ships were approaching their solar system, and should arrive within a week. Tom had been dreading this for years now and was not sure how to deal with it.

He told Asami he needed to go into the forest to mediate over events yet to come. Asami had learned not to question his odd moods at times and helped him prepare a light pack to sustain himself while gone. Tom stopped by the school and told Carl he had to be gone for a few days and for him to take care of his mother while he was gone. Carl told his father to be careful and not to stay gone long since his birthday was a week away.

The Future of Man

Tom went to the where the Ruins were once located and walked to where he remembered finding the sword and drove it into the ground. He sat Buddha style before the sword and pressed the medallion hard to his chest and closed his eyes. He first had Simon conceal his presence in case a hunter roamed into the area. Tom then asked Simon to present himself in human form, so they could talk.

Simon appeared in a dark robe with long dark hair and beard both shot through with grey.

"Tom, this is a form I once took when I once walked as a human on Earth. Does this please you?"

"It is fine Simon, thank you. Now I need as much intelligence on the arriving ships as possible. How would this best be accomplished?"

"Tom it would best be accomplished by going to meet the ships before they arrive."

"How can I do that?"

Simon just waved his hand and the next thing Tom knew he was standing on the command deck of a space ship amongst the ships' crew.

"Simon can they see me?"

"No Tom, they cannot. You can move though the ship without concern and from space to space within the ship without an open door. You are a ghost that cannot be seen."

"Thank you."

Tom was working hard to contain his own emotions as he observed the crew. They were deformed in many ways which made Tom wonder what had happened to humanity in the eight millennia

130

since he had left Earth. The language they used was unknown to him and was coarse nearly animal like.

He moved off the command deck through the ship to find one horror after another. But the one thing that nearly broke him was in the ship's galley. On a long-centered counter was a human body being butchered for food. He watched as another human was drug into the galley, and their throat cut, then laid upon another counter as life left the body.

These seemed to be normal humans in form they were butchering, and he moved back through the portal where the human had been led from to find cages containing more humans. There were male and females in the cages and they were like animals in their containment.

What he observed was beyond anything he could ever imagine with a male raping a female in one cage and in another it looked as if one of the inmates was eating the hand of a human. As he stood there one of the butchers brought in the unused pieces of a butchered human and tossed them into a cage. The inmates in that cage fought over the bits and pieces given them.

Tom could not take any more of this and moved out of the area to stand in a passageway.

"Simon, what has happened to humanity?"

"Tom, nuclear wars and over population has created this from what I could gain from their computer. Even as brutal as they are, they have a high level of intelligence to construct such vessels to traverse space."

"Simon, I cannot allow these creatures to find Haven. I have yet to ask this of you, but what are the limits of my power, or actually your power that I can command?"

"Tom, there is no limit to the power you can exercise, but I must remind you to use caution."

"Thank you for the word of caution. Send these ships into our sun. Let them see their demise and feel the heat as they are destroyed. If they have any link back to Earth, shut it down. Is this cautious enough?"

"Certainly. Do you wish to stay and watch or return to Haven?"

"I have no desire to watch."

Tom suddenly found himself back on Haven shivering from what he had observed.

"It is done."

"Thank you Simon. I need to rest now."

Simon once more gave a short wave of his hand and Tom slowly rolled over onto the ground and went to sleep. When the light rain came later that night, it never dampened the ground around Tom as if an umbrella was over him as he slept. Simon maintained his human form as he watched over him. He had a visitor during the night.

"Arthur, he is fragile."

"Yes Simon, which is why he was the best choice for this experiment."

"For you and the Council, this is only an experiment. For Tom, this is his life. You promised him no harm would come to him with this power you have given him, yet it is taking its toll on him."

"Yes Simon, once again we have misjudged the human species."

"No Arthur, you misjudged Tom. He was the type of human you were first searching for when it all began, but you continued to put them in position to be killers. I admire him his humanity."

"Simon, I do believe you are developing human traits."

"If I have, then I wish I had found them the last time you and I walked on Earth. Maybe what has happened, and I predict will happen, would have never came to pass."

"We both made serious mistakes then. Mistakes not even the Council could predict nor the effects of those mistakes. That is why we are allowing a human to control the powers we once used to control the experiment. So far the results are better than we hoped for."

"Yes Arthur, we made mistakes."

Arthur left Simon to continue watching over Tom. He told himself that once this was over, he would explain what he could, so Tom could rest in peace unless the Council silenced him.

Tom awoke several hours later to find Simon standing off to the side watching him.

"Simon, do you ever sleep?"

"No, I do not require sleep. But Carl is resting nicely in your bed with Asami."

"Thank you Simon. I have a request."

"I believe I know what you desire, but make your request."

"I wish to see Earth as it is today."

"Tom, are you sure you want to do this?"*

"No, but if what those ships carried is an example of what Earth has become, it needs to be fixed."

"As you wish Tom."

Tom found himself once again on a space ship looking down on Planet Earth through an observation portal. The once blue oceans were a dark grey and the polar ice caps were gone. What he first thought were clouds was smoke. Earth was ruined and there was only one thing Tom felt could be done about it.

"Simon, destroy it. Destroy it all. This cannot be allowed to move out into space and destroy other planets, or races they come in contact with."

"Tom, there are dozens of ships already out in space. Do you wish those also destroyed?"

"Simon, those are plague ships carrying a plague which can only be cleaned with fire."

Once again Tom found himself back on Haven.

"Simon?"

"Yes Tom?"

"Has it been done?"

"Yes, I felt it better that you did not witness the act."

"Thank you Simon."

"Tom, in a million years, mankind may once again walk on Earth. The planet will heal itself in time and once more be able to sustain human life."

"Again, thank you. I am going to set my tent and get some sleep."

"Rest well Tom. There is still much to do here on Haven."

Tom never responded to the statement as he went to the crawler and set up his tent. Sleep came quickly, but in his dreams, he saw a planet devoured by fire with even the oceans on fire.

Life Continues

Tom returned to his life knowing he had destroyed a world that was beyond saving. Carl climbed on Tom's lap after he sat down and hugged his neck and told his father everything was going to be alright.

Asami gave birth to another son and they asked Carl if he wanted to name the baby. Carl never hesitated when he said the new baby would be named Simon. This caught Tom off guard, but recovered quickly and told Carl he approved of the name.

Since there were no longer threats to the settlement and the residents had settled into a comfortable life style of hard work and rest, Tom had very little to do so he built a workshop behind their home and began to spend his time carving toys for the children of the community.

Technology slowly moved forward within the settlement as the small machines first brought to Haven were used to manufacture larger machines utilizing the metal brought with them from Earth. Soon that was not enough, and the Geologists and mining engineers went out looking for raw materials.

The evolution of manufacturing took two decades to grow as some settlers learned new skills from the older ones. In the community school, skills such as machine technology and wood working were taught to both sexes along with the mandatory classes in mathematics, biology, chemistry, English and Earth History.

Tom had required History to be taught and insisted that it was not to be doctored to make things look cheery on Mother Earth up to the time the Prometheus Expedition had left. He said the purpose was to teach the mistakes made on Earth, so hopefully they would not be repeated on Haven.

Simon was two when Asami once again announced she was expecting and this time gave Carl and Simon a little sister to fuss and watch over. She was named Yoshie as Asami had requested before Carl was born and like her brothers could be found near Tom while Asami was in her medical clinic or the hospital when not in school.

Tom first took Carl into the forest to learn nature when he was eight then Simon joined them when he was eight. Yoshie had to argue her case to be allowed to go when she turned eight and her logic could not be countered by the males of the family. This was still a wilderness settlement and every bit of knowledge could be lifesaving.

On Carl's twelfth birthday, Tom removed the box that Colonel Dubasso had given him at Houston and gave it to Carl. The box contained a silenced Ruger .22 caliber pistol. Tom was glad he had not had to use it on Pritchard and kept it for a time when it might be the margin between death and survival. Carl became proficient with it as he would hunt for squirrels or rabbits for food.

The settlement expanded as the years went by and other settlements were established closer to areas where the work needed to be accomplished such as on the other side of the forest where copper ore was mined. When Carl was nineteen, he led an expedition to the Northern Artic region and was gone for over a year before they returned having found a route to another continent.

The years of Tom taking Carl into the forest to learn how to live and survive in that environment gave Carl the edge on the expedition. They had used old crawlers utilizing the hydrogen motors and melted snow to provide fuel for them. This cut their transit time and the materials they had to transport over half of traveling by foot or by the newer crawlers requiring gasoline.

When Simon returned to what was now being called Haven, he had a new bride with him. Maria was the daughter of one of the Prometheus crew who was seventeen. A year later they gave Tom and Asami a granddaughter.

Tom changed his appearance once again when he had Asami cut his hair and shaved his beard. He also did something that had people talking in that Tom had a block of granite delivered to his home and sat in the back yard. He had it engraved with his information leaving his date of death open. He told Asami that this was to be his gravestone when his time was over. But the one thing that often-brought people by to look at the stone was that he had driven the sword almost halfway into the stone.

The medallion was hung in Tom's bedroom above his bed as he felt he no longer needed it to protect the settlement. Tom found peace making toys for the children including shipping large containers of toys to the other settlements as they grew. He was always surrounded by his children and grandchildren during his years as Asami continued as a doctor until she decided to retire after teaching others to take up the profession.

As with his children, Tom took his grandchildren into the forest to teach them how nature worked to the benefit of humanity. Even though he had separated himself from enforcing the laws of the settlement, he was often called to sit as judge on cases since he was trusted to be neutral and fair in his judgement.

As time passed, one by one the Morbius crew passed on to the next life. A special area of the settlements cemetery was reserved for this crew to celebrate their opening a new world. Tom watched as these old friends died knowing his and Asami's time would come. He hoped that he would go before her as he could not fathom life without her.

Asami had a stroke at age eighty-five and passed on three months later. Tom was heartbroken and withdrew into himself until Maria, Simon's wife had their fourth child, a daughter whom they named Asami. The infant seemed to give Tom new life as he tended to the child watching it learn to crawl and encouraging her to walk.

Tom suffered a massive heart attack at age ninety-seven and as he lay in his bed waiting for his final breath, he was visited by Arthur.

"Thomas Jenkins, it is time for you leave this life for the next. We thank you for your service to humanity."

"Arthur, I am ready to go."

"Thomas, you have already left that life and are about to start a new one."

Suddenly Simon was standing next to Arthur then another figure walked up beside Simon. It was Asami as she looked the first time he had seen her in Houston. She smiled at him and offered her hand to him. Tom eased himself out of bed and looked back to see his old body lying peacefully on the bed as if he was asleep. His children and elder grandchildren were to the side waiting for his time.

Tom looked at his hands and saw the muscles of his youth in them and his arms. He moved to where he could see himself in the rooms mirror and could see himself as he was when he retired from the Marine Corps with his hair cut close and dark brown.

He stepped to Asami, took her in his arms and kissed her before speaking to her.

"I missed you so much my dear Asami."

"I know my love, I missed having you next to me as we slept, but now we have eternity to be together."

Tom looked at Arthur and Simon.

"Simon, you once told me you had another name when you walked on Earth. What was that name?"

"I was known as Merlin."

Tom looked at Arthur.

"Then you must be Arthur Pendragon?"

"I was once Arthur Pendragon in another life. And you Thomas carry my blood in your veins as do your descendants. As long as there is a drop of Pendragon blood within the body of a resident of Haven, this world will be protected from harm. You were the last of my blood on Earth and you witnessed what happened to that world. Go now with Asami and live peacefully in the afterlife you have so richly earned."

Asami took Tom's hand and led him towards a glowing portal.

"Come my love, we had much to make up for that our old age would not allow."

About the Author

Leon Michaels is the author of several novels and short stories that reflect his twenty-three years of military service. Michaels enlisted in the Marine Corps in 1970 and has memberships in the Veterans of Foreign Wars, the American Legion, the Disabled American Veterans organizations, NRA, and Rotary International. In 1971, he married his high school sweetheart, raised three daughters and has three grandsons. He calls Creek County, Oklahoma home.

Made in the USA
Middletown, DE
26 November 2017